Amsterdam Angel

Amsterdam Angel

Jason Anthony

iUniverse, Inc.
Bloomington

Amsterdam Angel

Names and identifying details of some of the people portrayed in this book have been changed.

iUniverse books may be ordered through booksellers or by contacting:

iUniverse
1663 Liberty Drive
Bloomington, IN 47403
www.iuniverse.com
1-800-Authors (1-800-288-4677)

ISBN: 978-1-4759-5590-3 (sc)
ISBN: 978-1-4759-5592-7 (hc)
ISBN: 978-1-4759-5591-0 (ebk)

Library of Congress Control Number: 2012919389

Printed in the United States of America

iUniverse rev. date: 10/24/2012

For my Mother and Father

"Tell me, gentle traveler, thou
Who hast wandered far and wide,
Seen the sweetest roses blow,
And the brightest rivers glide;
Say, of all thine eyes have seen,
Which the fairest land has been?"

"Lady, shall I tell thee where,
Nature seems most blest and fair,
Far above all climes beside?—
'Tis where those we love abide:
And that little spot is best,
Which the loved one's foot hath pressed."

—Rumi

Special Thanks to:

My Brothers
Derek
Agata & Jim Van Haren
Michael Tubbs
Jennifer Dawson
David & Giovanni
Luke Pidgeon—cover design
Amy Van Haren
Karen Ingraham
Patrick Price
Art Weldon

1

Every summer my brother Joe and I watched with amazement as the sunflowers we planted in the spring sprouted and grew. We'd stand amongst them as they towered over us, stretching and reaching for the warmth of the sun's light so they could continue to grow.

Although Joe was exactly fifteen months older and just a hair taller than me, we were sometimes mistaken for twins, given that we both had blue eyes and wore our fine, straight brown hair in a bowl cut. Our mother also dressed us alike. In the summer our wardrobe consisted of brightly colored seventies-style track shorts and muscle tank tops, which draped our skinny frames. Winter wardrobe consisted of "Joe Cool" Snoopy sweatshirts and sweatpants. We were both big fans of Snoopy.

I always looked up to Joe, believing he did everything better than me. He ran faster, his art was neater, and at shared gymnastics classes he could do a round-off cartwheel straight into a back handstand flip with ease and grace. I stopped after the cartwheel, afraid to go backwards into the flip without the help of our teacher. And after I fell from the parallel bars once, I told my mother that I wanted to quit. Thus my gymnastic career ended, while Joe's carried on.

Our family's two-story home in Grand Rapids, Michigan rested atop a large hill that included its open backyard. Joe and I shared a bedroom on the lower level. Outside our room was a large playroom that opened to a deck overlooking the garden of sunflowers near the base of the stairs.

At the bottom of the hill, we had a sandbox, a swing set, and some monkey bars with a slide. Beyond, the land stretched into an orchard filled with cherry trees we would climb and snack from in the summer. Past the orchard was a long field of waist-high grass, perfect to hide or lie down in, and we could run freely from there into the open space that continued farther than our eyes could see. There was even a small stream to walk along and explore.

To us it was a magical backyard and everything Joe and I could possibly dream of needing was right there. There seemed no reason to leave. It was safe and loving there in the womb of nature. It was home.

Lying in the grass, Joe and I would also explore our imaginations by reading our series of "Choose Your Own Adventure" books. The words took us through the Amazon jungle, to deserted islands in search of treasure, on African safari, and to the ancient pyramids of Egypt. What made these books different from others was that at the bottoms of certain pages, they offered two choices followed by a page number. Depending on how we wanted the adventure to proceed, we'd turn to one page or the other, and the story would either continue or end. We'd repeat the process over and over, and this would allow us to go on multiple journeys within one story. We traveled all over the world in our magical backyard.

Some afternoons we would get lost in the world of nature and imagination for hours before proudly picking a bouquet of yellow dandelions for our mother. She always welcomed the gift with such a smile of joy before placing it in a small, crystal vase. She never let on that dandelions were weeds, not flowers. All Joe and I felt was her smile. And that made us feel good inside.

The back of our house served as the edge of a typically quiet suburban neighborhood where cars moved slowly while children played in the streets. But the road in front of our house was constantly busy with cars zipping by in both directions. Joe and I first experienced death when our dog died after running out into the street and being struck by a vehicle. A few years later, it happened again with our new dog when we came in from the magical backyard and neglected to shut the screen door. On the rare times we were in the front yard, the noise of speeding cars would spook us a bit—an occasional reminder that cars could hurt and even kill us.

Whenever a dog died my mother would get a new puppy, often of the same breed, and call it by the same name: Corky. It was easier on her emotionally to simply continue the life of "Corky". And maternal instinct wanted to protect her children from any pain.

Our older brother Jim was quite the opposite of Joe and I. His hair was darker and his frame more athletic. Jim was a sports boy and didn't care much for arts. He loved the outdoors, following our father and grandfather's passion for fishing and hunting. A true boy's boy, he didn't care if he was dirty, complained at bath time, and always wanted to stay out later playing with his neighborhood friends. The only time I saw him cry was when a Corky died.

When I was seven, our younger brother Justin was born. It was my first experience of new human life and being a big brother. I was eager to take on a nurturing role. I wanted to feed him, change his diapers, hold him, and then wait with wonder until he would get up from his naps so I could do it again. His nickname was Turtle because of the way he propped himself from his stomach sticking his head up to look around.

Although Justin looked more like Jim with darker hair and a rounder face, as he grew up he became a good mix of all of us. Joe and I were excited to do art projects with him. I would paint him with our mother's make-up and make him sparkle with her jewelry. When I discovered the art of photography at eight with my first Polaroid instant camera, Justin became my favorite model. Sometimes I used my stuffed animals as extras, but Justin was always the star. With Jim, Justin explored the world of sports. He seemed equally investigative about both worlds.

Our parents were both loving and supportive. My mother enjoyed a career in nursing, and she was able to draw upon her love of children when working with newborns in the hospital. But after Justin was born she worked less and gradually evolved into her calling role as a doting mother, wife and homemaker.

I never really knew as a child what my father did for a living or why he *had* to do it, which preserved life's magic that it was about fun and play. He simply wore a suit and tie everyday and did something for a company called Innerstate. I'd recognize the company's logo on the side of semi-trucks. It became a family road game to see who could spot one first.

When I was ten we moved to Ada, a suburb outside of Grand Rapids. My parents explained to my brothers and I about our father's new job and that it would afford a "better" life for us. The new home also had a backyard with a small forest. But through the tress we could plainly see other houses. I missed the magical backyard and the previous retreat and safety I felt. I even cried and begged my father one day to take us back to our old home. My emotions intensified when he expressed that we would never return *home* again. Life taught me the lesson that no place in this physical world is permanent. I had become a gypsy before even knowing what one was, always searching for the magic and comfort of idealized Home.

The new life amplified the conservative and sheltered teachings of Catholicism because of my father's new position. He began working for the Michigan Catholic Conference overseeing the benefits, insurances and retirement plans of the nuns and priests. We were invited to attend a mass by Pope John Paul II when he came to Detroit and when one of my father's associates was elected Cardinal my parents went to Rome for the ceremony and met the Pope. The picture of them shaking hands sat framed in our living room amongst our family portraits. I felt blessed through my parents' experience because I was taught the Catholic clergy were *closer* to God.

We were required to attend Catechism classes once a week and church on Sunday and all the holy days of the Catholic faith. The exposure to all the holy people made me feel I always had to be on my best behavior. That feeling intensified one summer on Mackinac Island at an event for company families. During the reception my brothers and I met one of the bishops my father worked with, who later become Cardinal. After my father introduced me to him, I shook his hand. He paused for a moment and looked me straight in the eyes.

"I can tell you would make a good priest when you grow up," he said.

I was a bit stunned and a little embarrassed as my brothers thought it was funny that I had now been *chosen.* I had always imagined a future family life with children but the bishop's words made me now feel I must be the priest in the family. A man who was *thisclose* to God had bestowed the priesthood upon me like a coronation.

My father's new job provided well for us as a family. The new house was even big enough that I received my own bedroom, but I'd felt happier sharing one with Joe. Having two separate bedrooms—even across the hall from each other—created more distance between us. And made it easier for each of us to shut the other out. The move caused me to feel a kind of stress that I'd never experienced before. I felt like I needed to find a place where I could belong and fit in.

When we reached high school age our parents gave us the choice to remain at the public school or return to Catholic school. Joe chose Catholic school and I followed a year later. I still longed for the memory of the magical backyard. Joe, on the other hand, chose to move on and in high school we slowly drifted apart. We eventually stopped sharing our lives beyond being civil. We drove to school in silence and spoke only if it was absolutely necessary. The silence affected me and made me wonder what I could have said or done to upset him. It didn't make sense to me. But I tried to remember that he did love me somewhere inside, *because we were brothers* as our mother had often ingrained. Those years made the memories in the magical backyard fade even further. A Once Upon A Time.

Joe continued pursuing gymnastics and later joined the cheerleading team. He was mocked for being the only male cheerleader, but he did not let it affect him. Perhaps he was hurt by their comments, but he never showed it.

As his brother, I was affected by the negative remarks about Joe. I just wanted to fit in. One evening our mother, Joe, and I sat down to dinner. They began playfully teasing me about something insignificant and completely harmless, but I took it personally and lashed out.

"Do you know what people at school are saying about you?" I said to Joe.

"I don't care," he responded.

I paused and thought twice about my next words.

"They think you're *gay!*" As soon as it came out of my mouth I knew I had gone too far. Being gay was a sin, and being called "gay" was the biggest insult we could imagine—something we did *not* want to hear.

My mother looked horrified at how I could intentionally be so hurtful to my brother. A silence fell over the table. Joe ignored my comment and appeared as if it bounced right off him. Staring at my plate, I sat there for the rest of dinner feeling guilt and shame.

Joe took the negativity and turned it around to the point of being accepted and even cool to be the only male cheerleader in the school district. His round-off cartwheel into three back-handstand flips before finishing with a backflip in midair across the gymnasium produced cheers and standing ovations every time. Joe never showed any signs of arrogance or that it was a big deal. I sat in the bleachers, one of hundreds applauding, doing my own backflips of pride.

While at the local community college Joe discovered his passion for dancing and with all his years of gymnastics was a natural. He transferred next to the Dance School at the University of Michigan. He was as good as many of his peers that had been studying dance from childhood.

After high school I attended Michigan State University. In my second year I pledged a fraternity. During my junior year Joe surprised me with a spontaneous call one Saturday evening to say he was on his way to visit me with a friend. When he and his friend arrived at my apartment I introduced them to my roommate. Joe was lively, funny, and entertaining. The apartment was filled with laughter, part of which was over me joining a fraternity. My brother showed genuine interest in my life and asked to see the fraternity house up the street. After the tour it wasn't long before Joe and his friend were in their car on their way back home.

"Your brother is hilarious!" my roommate exclaimed afterward.

I was deeply touched by Joe's special guest appearance and peek into my home, life and friends. As we approached graduation Joe and I began to share again.

Joe had several dance performances throughout the school year. Watching him and his fellow classmates move was ethereal. The dancers truly opened a gate to another realm where fantasy became life. They poured their passion into the art for each performance. I sensed the excitement of the inner child in their eyes.

In his final year Joe completed his dance thesis, which included creating a performance piece. He produced everything: choreography, costumes, lighting, and music. His piece was entitled "Daymares and Night Dreams". The dancer who was cast as the Dreamer cancelled at the last minute—so Joe played the part.

The show started with a spotlight on Joe as he awakens into a dream featuring an array of circus acts. The dream continued with two lovers romantically intertwined in a sensual dance. I found the entire work incredibly imaginative and creative—a whimsical glimpse inside the Dreamer's head. The power of the accompanying music evoked emotions that awakened my inner child, as well as my inner romantic.

After the show I waited for Joe in a back hallway of the theatre. It was crowded with many fans, both friends and family, waiting for their star to exit.

"Wow!" I exclaimed as Joe approached. "That was really amazing!"

"Thank you," he said with a radiant smile. "Thank you for coming." He invited me to a restaurant with his friends.

I could tell he appreciated that I came to support him on a Saturday night rather than going to another college party. But I was honored to be there. I was truly interested in seeing a glimpse of my childhood playmate's new life, just an hour away. With that night it felt like construction was complete on the bridge connecting childhood playmates to young adult friends and brothers. It gave a fresh start to a new relationship and I was happy. But before I made it across, the bridge collapsed.

2

"An artist is not a special kind of person.
Every person is a special kind of artist."
—Meister Eckhart

18 January 1998

"Have you done your resume yet?" my father asked. Justin and my mother sat across from us at the restaurant.

"Yes, I have one," I responded to appease him.

My last college semester had just begun. The previous night I partied late with my fraternity brothers then worked all day before driving the hour home from school. I was tired and not in a happy mood. I knew my father had good intentions but it wasn't a subject I wanted to talk about.

"Now is the time you should really begin looking for a job," he continued. "Are there any career recruitment fairs coming up at school?"

"I don't know," I said indifferently. "Classes just started."

"Well you should find out and get signed up. Whether you get the job or not, an interview is always good practice," he said.

"I *will* Dad!" I answered with an annoyed tone as the waitress brought out our food. I quickly ate and then excused myself. I just wanted to be alone. "I'm going to the gym. I'll see you at home."

Although exhausted from the day, I felt frustrated and needed to exert some energy. So I ran three miles on the treadmill. The more frustration I felt, the faster I ran. After relaxing in the sauna and hot tub I was in a calmer mood and drove home.

Walking in the door I could see down the back hall into the kitchen as I took my shoes off. My mother was leaning stiffly against the kitchen counter with her back to me. An unfamiliar and strange feeling brushed over me. Immediately I thought that I was in trouble. My mind raced, wondering what they knew. I had been experimenting with drugs with a few of my fraternity brothers and was terrified they found out.

I approached cautiously. Still, my mother did not move. I stood at the end of the counter; she turned and looked at me. Her expression was cold like a statue. I could not tell if it was anger or sadness. She had a lost look in the depths of her eyes. I knew something was horribly wrong.

"What? What is it?" I asked.

"Joe has been in an accident," she said softly. An image of him lying unconscious in a hospital bed hooked to machines rushed to my mind as I waited for more information. I felt like I was in a movie, as a gentle force turned my head to the next scene of my father coming around the corner. His eyes reflected immense fear. Time seemed to slow.

"D-d-dead. Joe died," was all he could manage to say.

A cold darkness penetrated my body, so intense and frightening. Time stopped and sped up again. The world around me as I knew it crumbled away and it felt like my entire being dropped into a vault of dry ice with walls one hundred feet thick. My eyes flooded in an instant. As my heart's tears made contact with the dry ice it changed the solid to gas, clouding and confusing me why this happened.

As my spirit tried to push on the dry ice vault the piercing sting it produced caused me to back off of death. The touch of death's dry ice produced a scorching and searing burn while my tears continued to change the solid mass into gas. It was a burn without the heart of a flame but with all of the pain. And the question of the unfamiliar and strange feeling I felt when I entered the house had been answered. Death had struck our home like a bomb out of nowhere and claimed one of our own.

My parents rushed to embrace me, but the love and warmth in their embrace was in vain as I was already trapped within walls of numbness. Love was a foreign feeling as sadness smothered it and anger enraged.

I broke away and rushed upstairs to my room. Pacing back and forth, I covered my face, crying uncontrollably. My mother entered. As she sat waiting on my bed, I tried to calm myself enough to speak. I needed to know more but feared facts would make the unbelievable nightmare real.

"What happened?" I finally said.

She took a moment and then spoke.

"He was driving to a class this morning," she began slowly. "The car slipped on ice and he lost control."

Tears began to swell again.

"He slid into the other lane and a pick-up truck struck on his side," she continued. "He was killed instantly . . ."

I couldn't hear anymore. The ice burn returned and I ran out of the room. I felt like I was suffocating and needed to leave the house, breathe some fresh air.

I rushed down the stairs to the back door and frantically began putting on my shoes.

"Where are you going?" my father asked from the hallway, my mother descending the stairs.

"I have to get some air," I said crying harder by the second.

"Jason," my mother pleaded, "just stay here; it's cold outside."

I tried not to look at them. I wouldn't let them persuade me from leaving. I needed to scream. Really scream. And I wanted to be alone to do it.

"I just need to go for a walk," I said.

"Take this," my mother said as she tried to hand me something warm to wear.

"I'll be fine," I replied, knowing I was only wearing a flannel shirt and it was snowing. It did not matter. Nothing did. I needed to leave *that* moment. I opened the door and ran down the driveway.

I had no gloves, hat, or coat but I was unaffected by the cold winter air. A fire of rage coursed through me. I hurried up the hill of the housing development, crying and slipping along the way. I felt strangely drunk with confusion, anger and pain. I wanted to escape my body and this world.

I made my way out of the development and onto a country road coated with a fresh blanket of snow. Without streetlights, darkness enveloped the night. Snow found its way into my shoes with each footstep. Still, I could not truly feel the elements of the world.

Suddenly I slipped and fell forward. I put my hands out in front of me, each one pushing through the deep snow, hitting the ground. I began to cry harder, the rage building like an active volcano. On my hands and knees, I stayed there for a moment. Tears dripped out of my eyes. Snot oozed out of my nose and saliva ran out of my mouth. My body felt weak.

When I stood up, I noticed lights from behind me. A lone car was approaching. I turned to face it, the white light blinding as it illuminated the falling snow that gracefully and ghostly floated down, blanketing the naked branches. I could not tell if the driver even saw me as he whipped passed, the noise breaking the night's silence.

As the car moved on, I let it all out. "Fuck! Fuck you! Stupid fucking cars!" I screamed as loud as I could as the pain of the ice burn struck. Hysterical anger swelled inside of me, an insane rage at every car in existence, the cause of Joe's death. I wanted answers. Immediately. Why? *Why!* Dead. I desperately wished it was me instead. Not Joe, with so many people in the world yet, to share his dance. Not Jim, who was living in love with his girlfriend, Christy, and achieved his childhood wish to be a police officer. And certainly not Justin, only fourteen, whose life was just commencing. I was the one in limbo. I moved from the childhood village, but had not yet settled in the adult kingdom. I didn't feel my life had purpose and was *certain* it should be me. Dead.

I screamed for three miles before returning home as the numbness—physical and emotional—spread to every cell of my body. That night I lied in my bed sobbing in waves as I heard hushed talk mixed with crying until dawn from my parents' room down the hall. There were moments of sleep. But they were soon interrupted when I cried myself awake, unable to shake the awareness of Joe's now forever-empty room across from mine.

The nightmare continued in the days that followed. A surreal and somber mood governed as we picked out a casket, made Mass arrangements with our family priest, and decided what Joe would wear for burial. Still I did not believe what was happening, that *Joe* was *The* Deceased.

The day of the wake provided the first dose of reality. The five remaining members of our family and Bushia, my mother's mother, were at the funeral home in the afternoon. Joe's body had arrived and was ready to be viewed. I was strangely eager to go in and see if it was true. There was simply no way that it was, because it made no sense. But I was equally afraid that it would be confirmed.

"You might want to hold on to your mother," the funeral director spoke gently to me, while stressing its importance in his tone.

My focus switched to my mother. Imagining her suffering. The last swing to her shattered heart was about to hit. I grabbed her with my right arm like two links in a chain. I was strangely afraid of touching her. As if the depth of her sadness could infect me. Terrified the light in her eyes would be dimmed forever. I locked arms with Bushia on my left and the director opened the doors.

Together we took baby steps into the room until the casket we picked out the day before was in view. Only now it was not empty. It was, our reality. One we would never wake up from. A truth so violent its initial collision threw us back and the breakdowns and unraveling began.

Bushia dissolved toward the ground. My attention went to her for a split second as I lost contact with my mother. She remained standing. Alone. She was bravely facing the truth of her child's final earthly duty, because she had no choice. We painfully moved further into the room knowing there was *nothing* that could be done.

There at the head of the room lying peacefully was Joe. Wearing the same light gray sweater with navy blue and red that we had picked out. The one he wore for his high school graduation picture, which now doubled its use and accompanied his obituary.

He was like a blinding light. I could not look too long with each glance as I shuddered. My mind saw Joe and yearned to go to him but my heart screamed that the stiff and lifeless form was not. My head and body began to drop into a fetal position. We all sobbed as the blow of death knocked us down. Like a familial choir of cries ours came out like another language singing, "Why? Why! Why?" over and over. An experience that was both tragic and mysteriously beautiful.

As I looked around, the room was surrounded in bouquets of flowers. The stunning arrangements helped soften the blow. I drifted to each, reading the cards attached, looking for one from my fraternity. I assumed there would be one. They were my "brothers". There were bouquets from each of my employers but nothing from the fraternity.

Leading up to the wake, we bittersweetly sifted through pictures to complete a collage of memories spotlighting Joe's nearly twenty-three years. I came across a card that he gave me for high school graduation. I saved it because it was touching and unlike the comedic cards my brothers and I typically gave one another. On the cover was a rainbow at the top accompanied by a poem from Ralph Waldo Emerson.

Success

To laugh often and much;
To win the respect of intelligent people
And affection of children; to earn the
Appreciation of honest critics and
Endure the betrayal of false friends;
To appreciate beauty, to find the best
In others; to leave the world a bit
Better, whether by a healthy child,
A garden patch or a redeemed
Social condition; to know even
One life has breathed easier because
You have lived. This is to have
Succeeded.

It was simply signed 'Joe'.

The wake itself was overpowering and glorious. The massive void that began the night and continued our new life was temporarily filled. Compassionate love burst throughout the packed room. Hundreds of people lined up around the building and slowly filed in from the cold January night, each patiently waiting their turn to say a few words or nothing at all.

But even without words, the heartfelt embraces and sympathetic eyes that flooded with light were enough. They sustained me throughout the wake as I floated from one gaze to the next. A reunion of long-ago-faces, some of which I never thought I'd see again, intermittently blocked the reality lying at the front.

The warmth in the room pierced through the frozen walls of my internalized vault, momentarily freeing me. But like a child afraid of the dark, I had become somewhat fearful of the light.

That night Joe's fellow dance students arrived at the wake and then came home with us to stay through the funeral. Over the days that followed, my family learned and felt how much Joe was a part of another family. The Dancers. Leading The Dancers clan Deborah, Joe's partner through many performances, and Nick, his sidekick. They spoke of the Joe they knew, melting theirs into ours. Death united two families.

It provided enormous comfort to my family and me to realize that Joe's impact had stretched far and deeply touched many. Their recollections depicted a happy, starving artist. A dreamer with a streak of reality working to carve out his path and passion. Perhaps he didn't have everything figured out, but he believed. And beyond what any one person or society said, he exemplified faith—trusting that if he lived the life that made him happy from his core, than a way would be provided. It certainly is not easy and requires enormous conviction, but that is faith.

In addition to faith, it takes great effort as an artist to control one's own fears, while gaining the confidence to go after a dream. Paul Torrence said it best: "Society is downright savage to creative thinkers, especially when they are young." But by living his passion Joe attracted a supportive family of artists living theirs and produced a joy whose light radiantly illuminates forever.

The love from everyone during those days inspired me to speak a eulogy based on the Emerson card. While examining Joe's life so quickly and intensely from childhood playmate in the magical backyard to Dancer, I recognized I had breathed easier many times during my twenty-one years. Joe had succeeded.

The Dancers brought with them Joe's possessions. Among his belongings was a book with a piece of paper inside used as a bookmark. Written on it in Joe's handwriting was an excerpt from a passage on death in Lebanese writer Kahil Gibran's "The Prophet". A poetic lesson to learn that was eerily apropos to Joe and the events taking place:

And when the earth shall
Claim your limbs,
Then shall you truly dance.

3

My mother should have suspected I was gay in kindergarten. Every time I went to school, usually in my signature outfit of Osh-Kosh overalls and flannel shirt, I would go to the easel and put on the oversized apron. All the colors of the spectrum were at my fingertips in old Campbell soup cans, each with a large bristled brush. I would paint a rainbow each time and proudly give it to my mother. Sometimes a sun shooting rays off or maybe a bird and a cloud would appear but there was *always* a rainbow.

It was the only thing I knew how to paint. The only thing I wanted to paint. And my mother seemed so impressed by my talent, proudly displaying my paintings on the refrigerator door. I enjoyed making her happy. So I continued to paint rainbows as my true colors shined through.

Long before my days of painting rainbows, labels had been given. From birth the label of boy was immediately attached to me. Along with it people around me and on television practicing the belief that boy falls in love with girl. Polish, Dutch and Catholic American Michigander were a few of the other labels I received.

Grand Rapids, described by one historian as "America at its best, a community of great expectations." Entrepreneurial Dutch and Eastern European immigrants whom created seventy furniture factories and 134 churches settled it. Most of the Polish were Catholic and lived on both sides of the Grand River, which ran through the city. The East side

Catholics and the West side. My mother was from the east side, her ethnic background 100 percent Polish. My father was a west side Catholic with a 50 percent Polish and 50 percent Dutch background.

The Dutch Catholic in me was through my paternal grandmother. But in the time of my grandparents it was frowned upon to marry outside your culture. Much like it was upon two men together.

So when my father's parents married, my grandmother was pressured to assume and learn the ways of the Polish. All Dutch influence was let go. A taste of that ancestry was limited to a Dutch style windmill cookie my grandmother always had in her home, along with an occasional trip to the springtime Tulip Festival in Holland, Michigan each year. But I was never exposed to Dutch food, music, dance or language, simply Polish.

At the beginning of first grade my parents took us out of the little public school we could walk to and even see from our front yard to give us a Catholic education. Our new school exposed us to religion throughout the week then reinforced it with mass every Sunday, and on all the holy days. A blanket of ideas of how one should live their life with the label of boy and Catholic was wrapped around me to absorb. Judgment and condemnation to any other way was also scattered in.

As a six-year-old boy I believed that what the Catholic clergy taught was infallible. My young mind was formed with the Church's declarations and beliefs about life. And I wanted to be a good boy and go to heaven. So the idea of love between two men vanished before it was even a thought.

There were also no gay couples or even a single gay man around me as role models to another way of living. The first exposure came from television in the form of Jack Tripper, the character played by John Ritter on *Three's Company*. On the show Jack pretends to be gay to make it more acceptable to his landlord who is uncomfortable with the idea of a straight man living with two women. The word "gay" translated as girly to me and I didn't want to be seen as girly. What it really meant got lost in the comedic shenanigans that revolve around the premise. It was portrayed as both something funny and to be cautious of like a circus freak. But I laughed because the audience laughed without really getting the joke.

Being gay got buried, much like my Dutch side. I didn't think or feel anything of it because I wasn't exposed to much else.

Until the buried feeling sprouted, in desire, on a holy day no less!

It was Good Friday and I was eight. I had the day off from school because of the holy day. But we were still taken to church, taught to be sad and genuinely mourn Jesus's death. The mood was always so somber and strange to be in church during the week. No music was played. The only sounds were the rustling of people moving in and out of the pews and putting the kneelers down and then back up again. Sometimes there were whispers of prayers or mothers telling children to behave if we were near someone. But there were typically no more than fifteen to twenty people in the vast church who usually gave each other plenty of space and stayed for different lengths of time. Some visited for only a few moments. Others, usually the elder, were there when we arrived and remained after we left.

While my mother prayed I watched various people sprinkle into the massive church to pray the rosary and light candles. In the front of the altar, propped up by the stairs, laid crucified Jesus in his loincloth. It was over six feet tall with His arms stretching a few feet shorter in width. Some approached the statue's front and kissed the wounds upon His wrists and ankles. It was seen and taught as a sign of love, remorse, and gratitude for this man who died for our sins, which I didn't really understand. I became drawn to the statue. Then a curious thought and wish formed.

"May I kiss him on the lips?" I whispered to my mother. Adrenaline rushed over me as I wondered if it was allowed or if I asked something naughty.

"Yes," my mother responded half still lost in prayer.

Like an African lion cub learning to rein in his playful, youthful excitement so he may gracefully move unnoticed through the night bush, I slid out of the pew and glided with each step to the near-naked man lying before me. But instead of my eye on the prey it was on an unchartered experience. When I reached the crucifix a streak of shyness shot through me over kissing His lips, so I bent down and kissed His feet. Then the boldness returned. I placed my right foot on the first step. Then straddled His chest with each hand as I propped myself up on the next step. Then quickly went in, kissed the man beneath me, and returned to the pew.

In the moment of connection with the statue I felt excited and refreshed like I had walked through a waterfall toward the rainbow it was creating. But in an instant, before I could open my eyes to see and feel the warmth of its colors, I was pulled back to the realm of the Church and all of its labels. It was my first kiss with a man who was not family. Someone who, ironically, was Jesus. The God who became man whom it was rooted in me to have a loving relationship with, kissed before God in His house before the altar.

And then the crushes began. Up first was pop star George Michael dancing on my television screen. As a pre-teenager I was fixated every time George jitterbugged across the stage. I wanted his blond highlights and feathered hair. I wanted his five o'clock shadow. I wanted his short shorts that showed so much and the hairy thighs that proudly emerged from it. I wanted to just keep looking at him. I wanted to look in his eyes when he sang directly to the screen. I thought I wanted to be like him, when really, I wanted him.

I did not understand or imagine that want in a sexual way. Or even as an innocent crush. I was simply attracted to the masculinity and energy that he strongly exuded. I shouted "Wake me up" and danced my own starring moment unbeknownst of its subliminal message.

After George came Rob Lowe. I was so intrigued in a naughty way to hear the words "sex", "video tape" and "Rob Lowe" all in the same sentence. As his scandal unfolded I looked at every tabloid cover in the checkout aisle with a picture of his naked body from the video. The places I didn't want it to be were blurred. But what was left to the imagination, I imagined. I thought of him naked and envy emerged for the two girls that were involved. But I assured myself I was just keeping informed of the news. Then I eagerly waited for the video release of his R-rated movie because there were nude scenes. When it arrived I replayed the scene several times, thinking nothing of being gay, but simply a teenage boy getting excited for a sex scene. That did have a woman.

But it was the return of John Ritter and his role in *Skindeep* that expanded my world of activities. In the film is a sex scene where a bronzed, muscular woman with long, bleached hair and a dominatrix attitude straddles John's character in bed. Although masculine in looks with a full beard and hairy chest, his character exuded a passiveness with his hands bound above his head. As her hands rose up his chest, so did I. But I did not understand that the feeling of masculinity being portrayed as passive was what aroused me.

As I repeated the scene, it surprised me that my body reacted so powerfully with excitement. My heart felt light and beat a little faster. My hand went down so naturally without a thought beneath the blanket. I placed my palm atop my erect member and pressed firmly down. Slowly, I instinctively began to rub my hand up and down, but never grabbed ahold of it. And when the hormone filled excitement reached a climax, an explosive eruption occurred. I was overjoyed. I had discovered a new hobby.

Before John I had wet dreams but I didn't understand fully what had occurred or caused them. Once I learned about masturbation, pleasure filled my nights with fantasies of adult males in my outside world. Shame always followed the escape, but never during. And denial was its shadow. Although my desires were filled with men I was conditioned that it was never allowed outside my head. That was firm—like a dictator's law.

In high school I played out the traditional experience of attending dances and escorting girls. When I arrived at Michigan State I was programmed to be a man and do what men do in college. From what movies and those older spoke of, it involved big house keg parties and sex. Not long after I started freshman year I attempted to complete those objectives.

One Saturday night I met up with a girl I graduated with and a few of her friends. We attended a keg party and became silly and drunk. One of the girls in the group was persistently flirting with me all night long unbeknownst to me. She had shoulder-length black hair that was thick with natural curls. Her emerald eyes sparkled. But I simply thought she was friendly and having fun. After wandering the streets we all ended the night at her dorm.

Soon her three friends exited, leaving us alone. She pounced and began kissing me. We drunkenly stumbled down to the floor below her loft bed. I was on top of her as we messily grabbed at and pushed the other's top up. Then helped one another unbuckle and unbutton our pants as if the world was ending while we sloppily kissed. First, a breast was exposed. I grabbed it while going down past her navel, to the top of her white panties that peeked through. I slid my fingers between her clothes and skin then husked her like a piece of corn, revealing my first close-up view of *a vagina*. I began to kiss and lick down there because it was what I saw in porn and what the explorer in me wanted to try.

But once I sniffed traces of female the latent gay man in me aborted the mission and came back up to her face. I then rolled, bringing her on top of me as we kissed, because that is what I also saw in movies. She started to go down on me and tugged my pants to my shins. Then she mounted me like a jockey and inserted me into her. As Jockey rode her eyes closed and her head went back while a concert of moans began. It kept me hard even while drunk to see her get so excited. Soon I wanted to be closer to her, so I sat up then rolled her onto her back. In the process I came out of her.

I started to press against her in thrusting motions that kept me aroused, trying to find the point of reentry. She soon assisted and guided me in. It was only after a few thrusts that I fell out again. I hadn't realized it and continued my intoxicated rhythm. Jockey sensed my inexperience then slowly squeezed herself from underneath me and started to put on her pants. So I began to put my clothes back on and thought we would still hang out. But she just looked at me, and did not say a word. However her eyes and her energy shouted *Go!*

It took a few moments before I took Jockey's hint that the race was over as the horse shamefully made its way off the track and to the door. And there sitting on the floor waiting outside were her three friends. Nothing was said but I felt as if they *knew.* In my mind I had failed to please a woman. And the embarrassment set in. I didn't even know if I was still classified as a virgin because I didn't orgasm.

But once was enough for me. The humiliation I felt was clouded by the fact I shouldn't have had sex before marriage, as I was taught. Catholicism became my crutch, a procrastination technique from dealing with my homosexuality. No sex before marriage. I didn't have to worry about sex. I was a born-again virgin only in college and nowhere near ready to get married. Problem solved in my head.

I found myself concentrating on "special" friendships with men; unaware it was really a crush. They were straight guys who were able to talk intimately of their thoughts and feelings about life. I respected the friendship for that and would not masturbate to them.

But sometimes I could not resist if I was drunk. I would voyeuristically imagine them with women and crave to be intimate to them in that way. I always felt guilty afterward and only repressed my feelings deeper.

One such friendship, during my freshman and sophomore year, was with a loyal Led Zeppelin fan with the heart of a hippie and an Italian background. He loved soccer and his small but fit frame proved it with sculpted calves and thighs. His wild brown hair was thick and wavy, and long enough to be pulled into a tiny ponytail.

We had a freshman astronomy class together, which was where the attraction to his presence began. In the beginning we sat in the same section of the vast auditorium. He usually arrived first. Soon, out of familiarity, he began sending me a friendly, welcoming vibe. So we started sitting next to each other in class but then realized we generally just got along too.

I didn't care for astronomy, but eagerly anticipated the class to be with Billy again. Unfortunately he rarely went to class after the first few months. As I sat in our usual spot, I looked with happiness for him to enter the room. If he didn't appear, my heart became heavy with disappointment. The later rare instances when he did make an appearance, amongst the stars in astronomy class with Billy was the only place I wanted to be. I felt a good relationship was forming, but as school ended, regrettably we lost touch and did not exchange information.

However, at one point he shared with me the apartment building he was going to live in sophomore year. In addition to another guy I wanted to form a "special" friendship we ended up in the same building. At the beginning of my second year I went to the gym in the apartment complex and was elated to see Billy working out with some friends. He recognized me and we began talking about our semesters' classes. We both signed up for a required English class. He spoke of his class with such interest and recommended that I transfer into it while the semester was still young. I unquestionably did.

Living in the same building and sharing a class facilitated the opportunity for us to spend time together. We shared homework assignments often in his room as he introduced me to Led Zeppelin and pot. His space was part of a three-bedroom apartment, but you needed to climb a tiny spiral staircase to get up to it. I felt comfortably tucked away with him, cherishing our time writing, sharing thoughts, appreciating classic rock, and getting high. The bed was always his spot, while I claimed the room's black leather chair. We usually did our assignments before we smoked, but sometimes after, and the writing reflected it. Then we would stay up, listen to music and at times pass out.

"You can just stay here if you like," he said one late night. "Then we can just go to class in the morning."

It was an offer I was not going to pass on even if it meant sleeping on the floor next to him. I hoped and successfully tried for other occasional nights sleeping over. It touched something pure and happy in me to be close to him. In the mornings before class we would sometimes smoke, which always caused a late arrival. One morning as we walked in giggling, our English teacher, Ms. Henry, crowned us with a nickname.

"Ah the Wonder Twins have arrived. Please have a seat," she said endearingly, shooting us a knowing look then tried to hide her smile and continue class.

I loved that she called us that. It made me feel closer to Billy, like kindred spirits. We both felt comfortable with Ms. Henry. She wasn't more than a decade older than us and although newly married, she kept her maiden name. With her long flowing skirts, tops in neutral colors, and her round frame glasses that hung half off her nose, she had the look of an intellectual bohemian. Her fiery red hair cascaded down her back, and her passion for literature and discussion was contagious.

Billy and I would go to her office hours with questions on class then usually branch off into other subjects. Her wide-reaching encouragement of all things reading, writing and life was addictive and inspiring. And then our bond grew even stronger when she found out I was from Grand Rapids.

"I live in Grand Rapids," she excitedly said at the connection.

"Really?" I replied in surprise.

"Yes, I commute on the days of classes. If you ever go visit your family for the weekend and need a ride to Grand Rapids or back to school, let me know."

The thought of sharing an hour car ride with my teacher was at first foreign to me. But it made logical sense and soon I took her up on the offer. She used the hour drive to genuinely get to know me beyond the role of student and her insight further encouraged me to keep writing.

My parents also recognized my pull toward writing and gifted me that Christmas with a beautiful brown leather journal. I began writing in it—the first of any type of diary—that Christmas night in 1995. Just after the clock struck twelve I wrote:

> *"Words can affect people so deeply—they are the essence of communication that bring about love, forgiveness and peace between people. It simply amazes me what words can do and the true power and magic they posses. This is why I want to be a writer. Writers can take words, arrange them and produce the power which affects people and brings about their emotions. This passion for words and writing has been brought about by an elixir that has truly opened my mind to an entirely new way of thinking and seeing things. A creative and almost magical*

> *sense of the world. It has definitely changed me inside and I am not the same person I was two months ago. I look at things differently and think more deeply about them. I don't know if this is good or bad, but the elixir has brought me a new view of the world . . ."*

Fearing my parents may find and read the diary I used the code word "elixir" to symbolize pot. It was never my thought that the elixir could be young love. I was taught that love between two men was not allowed, so it simply didn't exist to me. Whatever it was, I liked how it felt and I went with it.

The next semester Ms. Henry led a creative writing class and recommended Billy and I join. It became the highlight of my week to work on and share different pieces—both for class and personal—with Billy.

The new intimacy of sharing my thoughts through the art of writing made me feel vulnerable but excited. We read to each other our most personal thoughts. Most often Billy was the only other person who heard them. Although I knew he was straight, I felt uneasy and judgmental when he shared his sexual experiences. But it was still the first taste of real intimacy with a man. Sharing thoughts and emotions slowly began to turn my sexuality's closet doorknob.

In class, the writing love bug bit particularly hard one day while our desks were pulled together in a circle as we listened and commented on each other's writings. Creative sparks were exploding in the room when one of them slapped a dream into the back of my head. *I'm going to write a book.* But a question followed right behind it. *You're 19. What do you know about life, to write a book?*

I did try, with Billy as my muse. I wanted to write about two friends, two guys who had a great friendship. But I didn't get beyond picking names and writing a few paragraphs before my lack of confidence and something profound to write about stopped me.

That semester I pledged the fraternity. I hoped Billy would join me but he abhorred the idea, believing it was for people who needed to be told what kind of identity to have. As the semester became busy with class and pledging, our friendship changed. We still shared creative writing class but our time alone diminished and the friendship slowly faded throughout the semester.

The fraternity I joined was quite small in number with around thirty people. Most of the fraternities on campus were two or three times the size. In the previous years my house had not participated much with the rest of the Greek community. No single label for the type of guy in my fraternity could be given, like it could at others. We had an eclectic mix: preppy studious guys, bohemian potheads, heavy drinkers and partiers, athletic guys, and even one self-proclaimed redneck with a heart of gold. And unbeknownst to me and most of the others there was one gay guy. Everyone generally respected each other's differences and quirks. It was the fraternity land of misfit boy toys. The right fit for me.

As a pledge we had to choose our "Big Brother", someone who would guide us through the process and answer any questions. I was hexed by the charisma of a man whose nickname was Rex (Latin for "king"), as my Big Brother. His real name was Mitch but he embraced his Rex identity and acted as if he was a king of his own little world. He was a single child and it showed through his sense of entitlement.

Rex was "old" for a college student at twenty-five. After some devilry in the years after high school, his family convinced him to go back to school. He tried to be the wise, older guy in the house but he was playfully teased as the old man. Nonetheless, he was very charming and tall at 6'1" in his preppy clothes. His dirty-blond hair was slicked back and blanketed his legs, arms and chest, which usually peeked out from his shirt. His bright smile accompanied shining blue eyes. He won most people over with his alluring compliments and demeanor, especially the ladies, and me. I was attracted to his magnetism and wanted to form another close friendship. I hoped to learn through osmosis the qualities he possessed.

In reality, Rex drank and smoked too much. He was a business major who didn't take his classes seriously. A bad boy in sheep's clothing loaded with hidden insecurities. Eventually the truth behind the surface was revealed. But he tried. And he deserved an 'A' for effort.

But a spell was cast over me. I treasured our time together and heart-to-heart talks, usually when we were both drunk. And if I didn't feel like going home I slept at the fraternity house. Guys that lived in the house had a room, but also a bed in the dormitory on the third floor. I always slept in Rex's bed in the dormitory and it made me feel closer to him, while he slept in his room on the second level. Another unrecognized crush began. I would think of him sexually as the voyeur in the fantasies while he starred with a woman.

The summer after my sophomore year Rex lived in Naples, Florida with his girlfriend, who had taken a job there after graduation. I went down to visit him while on a hiatus between summer classes in July. It was the first time I traveled a large distance on my own with the ID of another fraternity brother who was twenty-one and I resembled. It felt liberating, the escapism of travel aided more when the palm trees and water became part of my world. My excitement and curiosity peaked as Rex picked me up from the airport and I wondered what *we* would do together and, for the most part, alone. I was far away from the realities of Michigan, college, the fraternity, or anybody else.

The first night, Rex, his girlfriend and I spontaneously decided to leave the next day for a visit to Key West. We excitedly woke early for the road trip to make the most of our day. Once we reached the bridge that connects all the Keys to the mainland, Rex allowed me to drive as he sat in the passenger seat and his girlfriend in the back. Any cares I had of past or future flew out the open windows. Peaceful blue water cradled us on each side as we rose with the arch of the bridge. It felt like rising into the sky on a single pathway through the air. The only sign of earth was each time the bridge descended and brought us back down through a Key. But once through, we raised again through the sky until reaching the very last one, a personal love of Hemingway, the quirky paradise of Key West.

I was in the moment like I had never experienced before. I vibrated at a different frequency that I didn't know could happen. The present was the only moment that existed and I surrendered completely to it and whatever lay ahead.

We found a little bed and breakfast on Duval, the main street lined with many bars and restaurants. The girlfriend got settled in as Rex and I went snorkeling. On the way to the boat he pleasantly surprised me by pulling out a joint, which we smoked on the walk. I was on a natural high as well as the induced one.

Afterward we rejoined the girlfriend and proceeded for the rest of the afternoon and night to drink frozen pina coladas, Sex on the Beach cocktails, and margaritas along Duval. Rex's girlfriend bowed out before the stroke of midnight while the King and I carried on, getting even more intoxicated.

Earlier in the pledge term word got around that I was a virgin, at least still in my mind. I was too embarrassed to share what happened with Jockey girl for another opinion. Rex had personally made it his mission to make sure I got laid. It was a subject I did my best to avoid whenever it came up with anybody.

"So are you still a virgin?" he asked as he took another sip of his cocktail.

"Yup," I said short and sweet.

"I don't understand."

"I guess I just haven't met the right girl."

"Well is there *anyone* you're currently interested in?" he asked.

"Not really," I said, feeling my underarms begin to perspire from the uncomfortable topic.

"Man, we have got to get you laid!" he said. "You just don't know what you're missing."

"It will happen," I said, eager to change the subject. "Hey why don't we check out another bar?"

"Sure," he slurred as we stumbled off our stools and onto Duval.

We had one more drink then called it a night. We could barely walk. Rex was slightly ahead of me.

We passed Bourbon St. Bar on our way to the bed and breakfast. As I passed my eyes locked on two spirited drag queens sipping martinis'. They were statuesque and curvaceous as they stood at a ledge outside the bar. One was a dark complexioned Latino that stood 6'0" with heels who wore a blond flowing wig with curls past her shoulders and a pink gown that sparkled and clung to a muscular body. Her partner in sass towered over her in heels at 6'3" or 6'4" and was much more slender with pale skin. She wore a blue gown that also sparkled with straight, black 1970's Cher hair that draped over each shoulder.

Each oozed confidence. With their well-chiseled jaws beneath their make-up I imagined they were just as handsome men as they were voluptuous women. As Rex and I walked by their radar zeroed in on a potential opportunity. And with a vibe both serious if we wanted it or a playful flirtation, a breath of nothing-to-lose was released with a catcall.

"Whewwwwwwww, wheeeeeewwwww," one whistled at us. I turned to look back.

"Looking for a good time boys?" the other called.

"Not tonight ladies," Rex answered, letting out a laugh as he continued to walk away. My look lingered at them, as their world introduced itself to me.

Soon I simply stopped and sat on the ground. It was my attempt to freeze time. I was in purgatory. I yearned to taste more of the drag queens' world. But without the slightest idea of what could happen. I also wanted to savor my alone time with Rex and wished for something more intimate to occur. Again not the faintest thought of what or how. So I waited, to see how it would play out. Rex realized I wasn't behind him any longer and turned around.

"Come on Jason, get up," he said as he started walking closer. "We're almost home."

"I can't walk anymore," was my excuse. But I just wanted to be out.

"Come on, get on my back then," he said while grabbing my arm and trying to pull me up. The idea of a ride on Rex's back was also appealing. So I got on and wrapped my arms around him. When we arrived to the steps of our lodging, I slid off his back and lay on the stairs.

"Jason, lets go inside!" Rex said with an annoyed tone. "We're just about there."

"I can't," I said with my eyes closed.

"If you don't get up I'm going to leave you here," he threatened. I didn't answer, pretending to be passed out. "Fine, I'm going up to the room, I'll see you in the morning," he said and then left.

It wasn't long after, while lying there alone, that I felt multiple hands sensually running over my body. I kept my eyes closed. The hands' touch soon became more erotic. One hand caressed my crotch; another slithered up my shirt like a snake. Then a hand ran down my leg and back up again to my thigh underneath my shorts, and squeezed. Another hand combed through my hair. I started to get very aroused and did not attempt to stop it.

"Mmm would you look at these hairy legs," the first of them said.

"I love that," the other said. "His skin is so soft."

"Don't you just love the young ones?" the first continued.

"How old do you think he is?"

"Oh he's just a baby chicken, certainly not more than twenty," the first replied. The rubbing got more erogenous.

"Let's see what's under here," the other said as he unbuttoned my shorts and took out my throbbing penis that eagerly awaited its first touch by another man.

"Oh my!" the first said with a juicy laugh. "Would you look at that!"

I opened my eyes to sit up a bit and saw my penis in the Latino drag queen's hand. She rubbed at a medium pace, which continued to feel good so I let it play on. The other concentrated on playing with my nipple.

"Well hello there honey," the other said. "What's your name?"

"Michael," I lied.

"And where's your boyfriend?" he continued.

"He's my *brother* and he went to sleep," I slurred as I closed my heavy eyes again. They continued to touch and stroke me.

"And what are *you* doing out here all alone," the first said. I drunkenly fluttered my eyes to spinning flashes of drag queen wigs, colors, smiling eyes and, my erect cock enjoying the summer night air.

"I . . . I . . ."

"We know sugar, shhh," the other whispered and I kept my eyes closed until I climaxed.

"Oh good boy . . . whoa!" the first said.

"Wow!" the other added.

The shock and shame of my first homosexual experience shot through me and I immediately began to pull up and button my shorts.

"Where you going honey?"

"Sorry, I have to go to sleep," I said as I pulled myself up. "Have a good night."

"Oh we did," they both said as the night burrowed deep in my subconscious.

As my final day in Florida approached, Rex asked what I wanted to do. I had heard he dabbled with different drugs in the past so I asked him if he could get anything besides pot to try. The explorer in me hungered for a new trip. I felt safe enough to experiment because nobody really knew where I was. He was surprised that I inquired, but open to the idea. Then with a phone call acid was produced.

Rex's friend who provided the acid suggested, without hesitation, that we go to a dive called Stan's on Marco Island for a Sunday afternoon. Without revealing any details, he felt it would be the perfect trip and it was only a thirty-minute drive from Naples. We figured out how to get there then dropped the acid along the way. About twenty minutes later everything seemed to get brighter and more animated. Tall, lean palm trees lined both sides of the road. At one point the trees' long palms turned upward and began to smile at me as we drove by.

"Do you feel anything?" Rex asked. "I'm coming up." It was new lingo to me.

"I think so," I replied, not knowing what I was supposed to be experiencing. "Are the palm trees smiling at you too?"

Rex let out a big laugh then took out a Marlboro Red and offered the pack to me. I slipped one out and put it between my lips. He flicked the lighter and brought it to my cigarette than lit his.

"Just sit back and enjoy it," he said as he rolled down the windows and turned the music up.

I reclined my seat slightly and took in the view for the rest of the ride. Rex kept a constant grin on his face. He would occasionally turn to "check in" on me, which caused me to laugh and said enough for him without a word being spoken.

Eventually the directions brought us onto a long, dirt road, then to an isolated building surrounded by dense tropical trees and foliage that looked very quiet from the outside.

"Are you sure this is it?" I asked.

"Yes, I'm sure this is what the directions say," Rex replied.

"Your friend wouldn't send us on a wild goose chase in the state we're in?" I asked with a slightly nervous laugh. I was starting to feel confined and wanted to be at the destination.

"No, he wouldn't," he said. "At least I don't *think* he would. Let's just go check out inside."

We walked in and the restaurant was empty, even though it was lunchtime, around 12:30. My gut sank a little before we heard relaxed tropical music in the back and discovered an outdoor seating area along the water. There still weren't many people there as we looked around. Maybe half a dozen. But their murmurs of talk hung in the air like an orchestra tuning their instruments before a concert. And of them all, we were the youngest people there by forty years.

"Sit anywhere you like boys," a vivacious waitress in her sixties with dyed red hair said as she squeezed past carrying food for another table.

We choose one at the center of all the other tables in the sun.

"What can I get for you boys?" the returning waitress asked.

"Grand Marnier, up," Rex said.

"Two," I replied, not really knowing what I ordered. I felt it best to follow Rex's lead on the experience and stay on the same level as him. He grabbed a fresh cigarette and passed me the box. Once again he lit my cigarette before his, which became our ritual and happened more often as the acid kicked in.

"I wonder why my friend sent us here," Rex said.

"I don't know," I said. "It *is* beautiful along the water and it's a perfect day to be outside."

"You're right," he said. "Want to go check out the water?"

"Sure." We got up and walked over to lean against a wooden rail at the water's edge.

"How are you feeling?" Rex said while flicking his cigarette butt in the water.

"Good," I replied. "Is it just me or is the water pulsating electric blue with lighting bolts of neon green and yellow throughout?" Again Rex just let out a big laugh, which made me laugh.

"Come on," he said. "Let's go sit down." When we arrived back at the table there were two snifters of Grand Marnier waiting for us.

"Cheers," he said as he raised his. "Thanks for visiting me."

"Thanks for having me. I really appreciate everything," I replied as we touched glasses. I took a drink. It was strong and my reaction showed it.

"Just sip it," he said with a smile.

We got comfortably quiet, as we absorbed the experience and chain-smoked. People slowly trickled in and filled the place up. I was glad we chose the table in the sun and cozily tucked into the center of the moment.

"I'm peeking," Rex said. More new drug lingo to me.

I must have been "peeking" too because the vibration of the place intensified. A crowd of people filled in—all—still forty plus our senior. But they were very young at heart and some, I could sense, were a little naughty and young at heart.

The majority of ladies had dyed hair and an abundance of make-up like turquoise eye shadow and bright red lips and cheeks. Their dentured smiles added sparkle, all perfectly straight and white. Clothes were colorfully salacious, providing comfort for the heat, but also sex appeal against their tan skin.

At times they appeared to have extremely disproportionate breasts or butts that seemed surreal and liquid like something out of a Dali painting. My perception of "senior citizens" never involved them laughing and drinking and dancing and smoking and mingling and having fun, all at the same time. And Rex and I sat chain smoking in the center. We connected with smiles and laughter while absorbing the carnival of sights and sounds around us.

Our sassy waitress regularly checked in on us as we switched to Coors Light. I didn't even think about ordering food. The thought of chewing and swallowing bits of anything seemed so foreign on the acid. It was as if I was only a mind and my body simply a vessel holding it. The single reminder I had a body was when I would have to pee. And even then the label of gender seemed non-existent in the moments of watching the liquid be excreted, the body like a car leaking fluids. I tried rarely to leave my seat for fear I would miss something.

At one point I looked over to Rex. He sensed it, turned his head, and then bent forward laughing in my direction. Confused, I turned around to see what caused such a reaction. There was a brightly colored blue parrot with some green feathers sitting on the shoulder of someone right next to me. I don't know what it appeared like to Rex but to see such a colorful creature while on acid so close felt to me like I was in space on a distant planet. The wise parrot knew all that was happening in my head and the universe and was revered as a leader. If it had opened its mouth speaking full and complete sentences I would thought it to be completely normal.

At the height of the trip, a skinny yet fit looking older man with a hand microphone appeared on a tiny stage fifteen feet ahead of us. His beard was virginal white and he wore sunglasses and a baseball cap. His rainbow colored Hawaiian style shirt had birds of paradise, hibiscus, and other tropical flowers all over it and was paired with white shorts.

"Good afternoon everyone," he began with excitement in his voice. "Welcome to Stan's! I'm Stan!"

The crowd erupted with cheers and applause. Rex and I looked at each other with raised eyebrows and big smiles at what could *possibly* happen next.

As the clock approached 4 for all the early birds, it wasn't simply a show, but a raunchy and risqué early bird show. Our jaws dropped for the next couple hours as we heard it all come from Stan's mouth; every curse word, every dirty joke or song, every sexually racy act or gesture I had ever heard or seen, especially from such a grandfatherly looking man. Then occasionally a guest would go on stage and reveal a little more than cleavage. And the crowd *loved* it and loved Stan. He was a local celebrity with CDs for sale. I had never seen anything like it.

As the show ended and the crowd died down, Rex and I remained a bit longer. I was still in pleasurable shock over the afternoon's events. Finally Rex motioned our waitress to come over.

"Bill please," he said as she pulled it out of her apron.

"Well did you boys enjoy yourselves?" she said with a cheeky grin.

"Unbelievable," Rex said. "We've had such a great day."

"We may be old," she continued laughing, "but we're not dead! And we still like to have a good time!"

"Amen! I can see that!" Rex said as he handed her some cash. "You put on a great show and I think you taught us a few things. Keep the change and thank you so much."

"Thanks handsome," she replied. "Now you boys come back and see us again. And tell all your friends!"

"We will!" we both promised.

On the drive home the sun began to set as we crossed the bridge back to the mainland. It was the perfect setting to end the day as the drug wore off.

"*Now* I understand why my friend sent us there," Rex said to me with a laugh.

"I hear you," I replied as he turned up the music and we enjoyed the ride. That night we nourished our bodies with a great meal before smoking a joint to come down and help us sleep. The next day I returned to Michigan.

I was so inspired by the trip and with traveling in general for weeks afterward. I wanted to quit school and go on the road somewhere, anywhere. The exposure to different ways of living life stimulated me. I made travel my priority. I believed there was something special out in the world waiting, just for me. A life that I could not even imagine at that point. A door had been cracked open, offering a peek of possibilities, while the force of society's way still pushed on the other side. Regardless, I took the first step with a call to my parents. They were each on a different phone and floor of the house so the three of us could talk at the same time.

"Oh hi Jason. How was your trip?" my mother chimed in warmly.

"Really great," I started eagerly. "In fact I wanted to talk to you about something."

"Go ahead," my father said, "we're listening."

"Well . . ." I began not really knowing how to say it. "I just really fell in love with traveling on this trip. I saw some different ways how people live."

"That's great Jason," my father said. "But I'm not sure I know what you're getting at."

"Well basically," I said, "I want to travel more, see other places. I'm not so sure I want to continue with my major . . . or with school . . ."

There was a pause.

"Right now," I quickly added.

"What do you mean?" my father responded. "What about your classes, your degree?"

"Well I'll finish my summer classes and then just take a break for a little while and explore," I said. There was a longer pause. I could feel my body heat rise from being nervous.

"Well why can't you just finish your degree and *then* travel?" he asked.

"Because I feel it's something I need to do now," I replied with an intensity inside as if I had been holding my breath for nineteen years.

"But it's harder to go back after taking time off," my mother said. "What if you don't finish then?"

"I don't know," I said. "I just feel like I need to do this now."

"You have to finish school first and get your degree and then travel," my father said gently yet firm, as he knew I would be disappointed with his words. "It's best to get your career going and then work from there." His mindset reinforced society's model for living life. Lacking the confidence in myself to imagine another way to live because the desire was so new, I respected his rule and made the choice to temporarily shut the travel door.

I was disappointed but understood he was just doing what he felt was best for me. But I wasn't going to let the travel dream go. I promised myself I'd follow through, after I received my degree. Even though my lack-of-a-plan plan was put on hold, with the help of Billy, Ms. Henry and Rex, seeds had been planted for my life.

When my junior year began and the fraternity charades and date parties with sororities occurred I played along dating girls. I would kiss them and put my hand on her breasts, because that was what I was logically supposed to do and enjoy. But I never slept with any of them—saving that of course for marriage, using religion to suppress my homosexual desires—which successfully played out for a year and a half until Joe's crash.

After Joe's death I was consumed by thoughts of him. Dealing with my sexuality didn't exist. Intercourse with a male or female was not considered. All I needed each day was one reason to continue to the next. I also had a lot of questions that required more solid answers through personal experience, instead of what someone told me.

There were two main teachings that Catholicism taught me to believe from birth. First, that there was a heaven. With desperate, hopeful sadness I vehemently held onto that teaching when Joe died. We *would* be together again. Now I longed for proof through experience of this *next* world. That Joe was still there. The second teaching preached that homosexuality was wrong. This knowledge provided me a more difficult challenge to correct.

A week after the funeral I went back to school. I was hurt and hesitant to remain living in the fraternity house after no support through Joe's death was expressed. A ray of darkness made of rage photosynthesized to feed a little seed of hate growing inside me. I was advised by the collective of Everyone, to get back into my studies and work, just keep busy, because I was so close to finishing. So I took the only advice I was given . . . while I wished I could take a big break from life.

My busyness consisted of going to class, to the university newspaper to work, and then I'd drive to the health club. It was in the car on the way to the club—confined and alone—that the ice burn would return. I would allow myself to cry for the 15-minute drive. I was so tired and exhausted of crying. When I arrived at the club I ran my frustration and anger out on the treadmill until I was depleted. The gym was followed by dinner and then usually the bars, getting at least buzzed if not drunk every night.

On the way to the gym I would listen to some of Joe's cassette tapes that I found in his no-longer-needed earthly belongings. One particular drive the usual tears were dropping and my attention was not on the music until a deep, raspy voice struck me. Louis Armstrong was serenading "What a Wonderful World". I couldn't see how it was a wonderful world in any way. But the beauty in the song touched and surprised me with a different side of Joe. My memories were of Michael Jackson, Madonna, Prince, Whitney Houston and George Michael singing out of his room growing up. Now Louis's "What a Wonderful World" forever connected me to Joe whenever I heard it.

In the beginning I only thought of death when I thought of Joe. There was such a sad void in the first week that memories of him became a black hole. But as the weeks passed I was flooded with memories from childhood on, both good and bad. Some were so obscure that I don't think I ever would have remembered them had Joe not died.

With that came the concentration on all times I fought with Joe or memories that could have been. One missed memory that I obsessed about happened weeks before his death. The film *Titanic* was released and my family went to see it one night after dinner. I'd already watched it the week before and stayed home, alone. After Joe's death it bothered me that I missed an opportunity for one more shared remembrance to cradle, because there would be no more, ever.

A few weeks after Joe died The Firsts without him began so I went home often to be with my family. Three weeks after his death was our mother's birthday and a week later on Valentine's Day it was Joe's. As I turned into the cemetery on his birthday, Celine Dion began singing "My Heart Will Go On" on the radio. I had not really listened to the lyrics closely before but did in that moment.

The song resonated with Joe. And just as I pulled up to his gravesite, the last note played. The timing that the song stopped just as I arrived was noted in my mind. But just as quickly, the reality of what remained of his physical presence beneath the frozen ground smacked me harder.

After Joe's birthday came Jim's. The month ended with a dance performance that Joe was originally scheduled to be in at the University of Michigan. It was dedicated to him, and my family and I attended. The month left me exhausted on all levels as I kept up with class, work, and bar life. I was fortunate to have two jobs that paid well for a college student and allowed me the luxury of going out often, with a good friend by my side.

Dallas, whose real name was Matt, was the only friend I opened up to at school about my brother. He was a year behind me but we were pledge brothers for the fraternity. He moved into the attic that semester. My room was a floor below. Raised in a privileged, Dallas Jewish family, he, similar to Goldilocks, didn't like anything "too hot, too cold or too wet." He was very fond of air conditioning in the summer and being cozy and warm in the winter. Comfort was key.

His face angled to a point with rounded edges and had full cheeks that any grandmother couldn't resist to grab and squeeze. His brown eyes normally matched his hair. But he was experimenting with a new look—one he wanted to try before the real world—and now sported spiked bleached hair accompanied by a tongue ring to complete the look.

He approached new experiences and the unknown, such as our pledge term, both with curiosity and timidity. It made him often want to explore it together with someone. But when he discovered that the challenge or experience was not difficult or nearly as scary as he imagined once on the other side, an inner child of joy came forth with the accomplishment. His heart was big and good.

He made me laugh long and hard. When he was feeling confident, a very blunt and direct humor would come forth. Even his laugh made me laugh—eyes squinted shut, mouth open wide and head tilted back with a boisterous and vibrating sound coming out.

Dallas helped me pack my car the early morning, a day after Joe's death, when I returned to school for some clothes. Although not much was said, his actions spoke louder than his words. I could feel his heart was heavy for me.

"I've had grandparents and older people die, but I just *can't* imagine if my brother died," he said.

I sensed he really went inside his head to explore what I had described, as if it had happened to him. We shared entering the fraternity together and experimented with drugs together so I felt as if his spirit latched onto mine and said, "so we'll go through this together too."

Dallas's upper class allowance allowed him to go out with me all the time. We shared a love for eating out and went to restaurants each night for dinner before the bar. Some nights I would come home drunk from the bar and the ice burn would return. Dallas was always there during difficult moments no matter the time of night, even if he didn't know what to say.

Although I went to the bar for some laughs and drinks before Joe's death, afterward, I was unaware that behind the laughs I was drowning the pain the ice burn caused. I numbed and avoided it to maintain my course toward graduation. I did keep a promise to myself, made before Joe's death, to travel afterward. Despite the daily drinks and dinners I still planned and saved money to take myself to Europe and do the sites before I joined the real world. But there was no plan or direction that followed.

While friends around me were preparing their resumes and setting up interviews I felt miles behind. I was still trying to comprehend what happened. The home environment of a fraternity house with people coming and going did not provide the stability and quietness I needed. My parents and Justin were together to heal, and Jim had a home with

Christy. My house was not permanent. My physical life didn't include three brothers anymore and in a few months time it wouldn't include the house I was living in or life I was conducting. There were too many factors outside of me that had no longevity. I felt like an orphan about to leave the orphanage in quest of a new home.

Life's merry-go-round sped up. I wanted to hold on but was having trouble staying put. So I got off to wander, and look for a new playground. And the pursuit took me to Europe.

4

My youthful sense of immortality was deeply shaken with Joe's death. If he could die at twenty-two then I too could leave the world at any moment. Tomorrow could no longer be taken for granted. So I decided to do everything I dreamed of doing. And I dreamed of exploring as much of the earth as I could before it was my time to go.

Upon finishing one final summer course before officially graduating, I flew to Zurich, Switzerland in August 1998. With money put away, I planned to travel for two months. The morning I arrived I was exhausted from the eight-hour flight. While I waited for my luggage, I heard, for the first time, another language being spoken over the intercom. It reinforced the reality that I was in a foreign country. I collected my backpack, passed through customs, and then was finally able to go outside into the fresh air. Once I reached the curb the culture shock of conversations and signs all around me in Swiss German slapped me in the face. I was frozen with fear and every minute felt like twenty.

"Mister, mister," a taxi driver said as he approached. "Taxi?"

All I could do was shake my head. I just needed to sit for a moment.

Oh my God! I thought *I'm here for two months! What do I do next?*

But then like any journey beginning with the first step, the next taxi that approached, I took.

Originally I planned a nice, neat spherical path around Europe visiting the countries that interested me. From Zurich I intended to go south, through Italy, across to Greece, then head north. Followed by Hungary, The Czech Republic, Germany, and The Netherlands before ending my travels in France. But four days into my exploration the circular course met a detour.

It was mid-morning in Interlaken and I was part of a group of twelve travelers driving up toward the Swiss mountains to go canyoning. Along narrow roads the two shuttle vans carefully ascended as we passed grazing cows and postcard pretty cottages scattered about with the white cross and red background of the Swiss flag flying.

Although from many different countries, the group all matched wearing black wetsuits and yellow vests. Our heads were topped with yellow helmets that humorously christened us with new names written in capitalized letters with black marker. Our new monikers included "BIFF", "BUFFY" and "SPIKE". I was "ZURI".

After driving through a forest of trees atop we disembarked for a small hike to a cliff. It dropped about fifteen feet into a small pool of water with the circumference of a child's wading pool. Jagged pieces of mountain surrounded its edges. As the summer sun melted the snow from the peak the water ran down and created scenic waterfalls.

Then the guides gave a lesson on how to *jump* off. It wasn't the height of the cliff that scared me, but rather our guide's insistence to enter the water at the *exact* spot he instructed. The pressure didn't end with hitting the bull's-eye. It intensified. We also had to remember to bring our knees to our chest before reaching the water. Otherwise we'd risk injury on the unseen rocks below because of the shallow depth. The guides had every pool figured out like a mathematical formula.

One-by-one I observed a few people jump. Everyone squealed like giddy schoolgirls, applauding and cheering with each successful splash. When it was my turn I slowly inched closer to the edge. I took a moment and examined precisely where the guide pointed to land. Then repeated the directions in my head. I took a deep breath and jumped. Adrenaline began to rush with each inch I fell. I closed my eyes and brought my knees up just before I hit the water. I submerged before bobbing back up, relieved to be alive.

The water retained the coldness of the mountain snow. It immediately woke me up and eradicated any remaining jet lag. I felt officially baptized

Gypsy. Every aspect of the nature before me—the rocks of the mountain, the brisk water, the land, the trees, and the plants—emanated a pristine and fresh crispness. There was a sense of delight and accomplishment like when a child takes his first step, realizes he did it, and that it wasn't as frightening as imagined. And I was ready for more.

From that moment, there was no way to go but down. We continued to jump cliffs, slide with the waterfalls, or repel. I understood why I had never heard of canyoning. America's stricter safety regulations wouldn't make it legal. The danger made it more thrilling, while "BIFF" from the group made it sexy.

BIFF was a tall, slender man in his twenties with a deep, dark tan, brown hair and eyes, and a ripped body. He was an American studying abroad all summer in Paris and was now traveling for pleasure. BIFF's excitement was electrified. As if he and Mother Nature were epically making love, having multiple orgasms with each feat. To hear it was hot, contagious, and drew me to him. He was straight but I was extremely attracted to him and the adrenaline filled challenges were bonding. I wanted to form another "special" straight friendship with a guy.

The group celebrated our adventure with nature that night with drinks at the activities center where we began the journey. The mountains surrounded us and were lit with full moon. The next day BIFF and I both signed up for bungee jumping from a gondola in the mountains. On the ride back he mentioned catching the next train out to the French Riviera. He had been there before and spoke of it with such relaxed, glamorous beauty. His first-hand account enlivened all that I had seen and heard of in the movies growing up.

"Wow, sounds amazing," I said. "I had not planned on visiting the French Riviera."

"Come along if you like," he said. "I just have a day before I return to Paris. But I'll show you some of the beaches. Do you have your bags with you? We have to go straight to the station as soon as we get back to the hostel if we want to catch the train."

The thought of spending more time with BIFF, even if only for a day was worth it. The fact that we would be half naked on the beach was enough to break my circle itinerary, although I probably would have gone to Siberia if he led the way. Life's class was beginning and the lessons "Follow Your Heart" and "Go Through Open Doors" were on the syllabus.

After returning to the hostel I raced to get my bags. We got to the station just in time to jump on a train to Geneva. From there we would take a night train to Nice. With the spontaneous decision to join BIFF I began to learn that sometimes in traveling, whether on vacation or in life, the best plan is no plan. I threw my nice, neat circular path out the train window.

It was worth the one-day date with BIFF. Through his abroad program he learned enough of the language to aid his experience. He taught me basic words for food and how to order, as well as phrases for traveling and train talk, what to look for at the stations, and on the boards. His tips for traveling saved me hours.

My first attempt at train travel was going from Zurich to Interlaken. I spent two hours getting *out* of Zurich, only to go the wrong direction. After backtracking, switching trains in Bern and going the right direction, I arrived to Interlaken six hours later. It should only take two.

BIFF also showed me how to travel in comfort on the night trains. For instance, climbing into the luggage racks above to stretch out for a better night sleep, instead of remaining in the uncomfortable seats that barely went back. He was the best type of guide to have: hot, kind, eager to help, and all mine.

Upon arriving in Nice BIFF found me an inexpensive pension, speaking French to the man behind the desk to make sure I would not get ripped off. It was a small, simple room not far from the main promenade along the beach. My window faced other buildings with an alley below. But it gave me a chance to have my own room and space from the hostels.

After getting settled he took me to the Picasso Museum. BIFF had already been but was keen to go again and show it to me. I was a puppy dog, happy to follow wherever my master wanted to go. For his part, he was enthusiastic to teach someone and share the places he liked.

After the museum we went to an open market to pick up some food for the beach. The tables stretched beneath large tents were filled with the freshest and most colorful fruits whose smells seduced the sea air. It was an Eden of Fruit perfect for the heat of the midday sun that approached ninety degrees. I bought some perfectly ripe peaches to take with me.

Our first stop was the beach in Antibes. I pulled out my large tapestry sheet big enough for both of us to lie on. As we sunned BIFF reminisced about the last time he was in Nice with his girlfriend. He pointed to an area in the water while fondly describing it as the spot of their exhibitionist sexcapade amongst other swimmers. I voyeuristically imagined what it would be like to have sex in the open water, envious deep down of how lucky *she* was to have had such a hot and sexy time.

Then BIFF went into the ocean, bringing the half of my visual that I needed and wanted to life. I watched his wet body glisten in the sun. While he emerged in and out of the water I sunk my teeth into each succulent bite of juicy peaches, titillating as many senses as I could.

The sultry sun sustained my mirage man oasis. But time was not kind as the hours flew away and too soon my mirage man had to depart. I took a cold shower. Then explored Monaco the next day.

From the Riviera my journey began to scribble all over Europe, coloring it in with different experiences depending on who I met or what I had heard from other travelers. I felt sucked into a current. The "Choose Your Own Adventure" books Joe and I read as children sprang out of my imagination and anointed me protagonist. I never knew what was going to happen next or where I would go. I was a free spirit floating along.

But along the way there were many signs of Joe as the ice burn returned. Whether I saw street performers dancing or heard his name, there seemed to be gentle whispers woven into the days. Seven months had passed since Joe's death but he was on my mind every day. Reminders of him saddened me making me feel far away from my family and sometimes very lonely.

But traveling Europe was my big dream that I tried to honor and be grateful for the privilege. Along the way I posed alongside legendary structures like The Colosseum and Berlin Wall. But at times I felt like a robot tourist, snapping my photos with the famous sites to simply check them off The List.

The random places and no-agenda aspects of my trip were far more visceral. Such as discovering Gaudi's La Sagrada Familia in Barcelona and climbing its towers like a kid playing in a fortress. They awakened the traveler in me to touch, be touched, and connect on a deeper level. The English writer G.K. Chesterton expressed it best by saying, "The traveler sees what he sees. The tourist sees what he has come to see."

Three weeks into my trip I was walking around a square in Salzburg with a view of the castle overlooking the city. Scattered around the square were artists selling their crafts. I approached a painter whose art consisted of the silhouettes of dancers. Some on display showed a male dancing with a female, females dancing together, or simply a single female in a dance pose.

The pieces exuded gracefulness, simplicity and, for me, Joe. I was reminded I'd never see him dance again. My heart sank like an anchor. Still, I was mesmerized by the paintings because I felt Joe. So I decided to purchase one for my mother. Flipping through the canvases leaning against one another I searched for one of a lone male dancer.

"Just male?" I asked the painter while pointing to the male figure in one of the coupled pieces.

"Man, yes," the artist nodded, then continued showing all the paintings with both a male and a female.

"Yes . . . ah . . . only *one man* in painting?" I held up a single finger determined to find another way to express myself. "Like this," I said, picking up a painting of a single female, "but just man." I pointed back to the male figure.

"Ah, sorry, no," he said shaking his head. Then directed me again to the couples, attempting to make a sale.

"Thank you," I said. "They are very nice but *I want just one man.*" I smiled politely and he returned a smile. I left feeling disappointed and saddened. But the image of his silhouette dancers stayed with me.

After the first month I traveled to The Netherlands for my first date with Amsterdam. It immediately romanced me with its quaint arched bridges which lit up at night and stretched over the rings of canals that cradled me. The tall 17th century homes that stood shoulder to shoulder with decorative gable tops and large narrow windows that lined the canals combined with the cobblestone streets produced a fairy tale feel. I stayed a week waiting for my former pledge brother Dallas to reach England. The school year was beginning and he planned to study abroad for a year at the University of Surrey in Guildford, a town an hour south west of London. We intended on meeting up somewhere in Europe. Although my original plan didn't include England, I did not anticipate how much I would long to see and be grounded by a familiar face. So I decided to go to England the same day he arrived and surprise him.

I only had the name of the town and a phone number to the school to contact him. Upon arriving at the train station in Guildford I discovered signs directing me to the university. It was Friday with five o'clock looming. I hoped to speak to someone before the school closed for the weekend. I found an administration building and approached a man behind the glass.

"Hi," I said. "My friend is studying here this year and he arrives today. I have been traveling and wanted to surprise him. I called a number he gave me to find out where I could locate him, but they said their computers were down. Can you please tell me where he is staying?"

"I'm sorry," he replied, "but it is school policy not to give out any information on students for their safety."

"Well is there any way I can contact him or leave a note so he knows I'm here?"

"You can leave a message in his mailbox."

I figured it was a long shot and didn't expect Dallas to check his box on his first day there. But I didn't have many options. I left him a note stating I was in Guildford and would wait at the Student Union. My surprise was ruined. But I was now more concerned that I didn't know the town and had not seen any hotels as dusk approached.

I went to the Student Union and waited inside for five minutes before giving up on the idea that I was going to meet Dallas. It was time to figure out where to sleep for the night. I gathered up my bags and walked out the door.

As soon as I left Dallas came around the corner and right toward me. We looked directly at each other and it registered as natural for a split second because we knew one another. Then complete shock brought him to his knees.

"What are you doing here!" he exclaimed.

"I came to surprise you," I replied with astonishment.

"Well you did!" We rushed to hug one another.

"I didn't know how to get a hold of you and thought I was going to be sleeping outside," I said.

"I was just heading back to my room after getting familiar with campus. Then realized I had not been to the Union yet," Dallas said.

"Am I glad you did!" I responded now laughing with joy.

That night we hopped on a train to London for a celebration reunion. Even being so far away from everything I knew it felt grounding to be with my good friend that I turned to after Joe died. Meeting up with Dallas felt like he kept his commitment to go through Joe's death together, just when I needed him. No matter where I was in the world. After all the reminders of Joe and lonely moments in the first month, like the first time, Dallas was once again by my side. I didn't care then about traveling around or seeing anything else. I just wanted to stop, rest, and be with my friend.

I stayed with Dallas for ten days. By then I felt recharged and ready to explore new countries for my remaining weeks in Europe. We traveled to Amsterdam together before his classes began and found a place to rest our heads at The Globe hostel near Central Station. We then indulged like pigs in mud, making appearances at numerous coffeeshops, trying all the different weed, hash, space cakes, cookies, and shakes.

Usually afterward, feeling high and silly we wandered to the red light district. My previous visit I treated the area, like many, as a tourist attraction to simply walk by and gawk. But it did have a function. And with Dallas's nonchalant lead I curiously followed him *into* a sex shop, eager to explore the porn booths.

We walked up and down the maze of aisles looking for a green light on the outside, which indicated a booth was open. After taking a peek in to make sure it was fairly clean we entered for our private moments of porn.

Each booth was the size of a small closet and accommodated one person. It was dark inside with a little seat to the right. The only light was from the television screens.

To the left was the main screen twelve inches wide. It displayed the porn of the spotlighted channel while four smaller screens above it, arranged in a square, showed additional video options.

To the right of the screens were the controls lit in red, including four square, chunky buttons, lettered "A" "B" "C" or "D". If pushed, the smaller screen linked to that button would transfer to the big screen. There were also two rectangular buttons with black arrows facing up and down. They switched the variety of videos, over twenty in total, forward or backward. Finally two square buttons controlled the volume. Usually I kept the sound up. But if I heard the door to the next booth close, I would be respectful of my neighbor and turn the moans of pleasure down.

After sitting on the little seat and inserting my Guilders into the slot the porn started as the timer's red numbers counted down. It was while flipping through the channels that my Little-Boy-from-Michigan's eyes saw just about everything: traditional straight sex with two, three and groups of people, men with animals, women with animals, fetishes and S&M. There was a whole lot of sex and orgasms happening in the little closet.

But it was when my eyes, for the first time, saw two men having sex that the channel surfing came to a screeching halt. A burst of colorful excitement erupted within me. I felt so safe, alone in the booth, as I dove headfirst into the new world on the screen before me. Many Guilders and minutes were spent in my closet.

Eventually I heard Dallas outside calling my name. I waited until I sensed he passed, fearing if I came out while he was near my booth he may hear or see my choice of indulgence. I also wanted to get my money's worth and finish my business. Once I did, I slipped out; making sure Dallas wasn't around, and then went to find him.

"Where have you been?" he asked.

"Where do you think?"

"Right," he said laughing. "You done?"

"Yup," I said.

"Good, let's go find a coffeeshop."

So we would go about our day's and night's strolling around the city. And when our wanderings took us by another porn booth shop, either his horny desires or mine led us in, as we became regulars at each one. My second date with Amsterdam I discovered another layer of happiness and excitement knowing I had access to *that* world. It was in a way that was comfortable and enough for me.

Gay porn became my educator for Homosexual Sex 101, teaching me different techniques of what to put where and how. It also jump-started my sex life again, with myself. But still I did not think of myself as gay because it remained in the booth and unknown to anyone in the world but me.

When Dallas returned to England I traveled south. The temperature was dropping as autumn approached. After a weekend in Budapest I set forth on a thirty-six hour train ride to Athens. Greece was cut from the original plan, but found its way back on the itinerary. I felt the urge to relax on the beach and soak up any remaining summer before taking on Paris and returning to America.

After touring the Acropolis I walked back down the winding cobblestone streets. Joe again was on my mind. I had been alone since leaving Dallas and yearned for a good conversation with someone.

I discovered a little gift shop on a corner and entered. It was cluttered with many tourist gifts, a duster's nightmare. Miniature statues of various Greek gods and mythological heroes filled many shelves along the walls from floor to ceiling. Packed cabinets and tables were scattered around the floor. It was a place a mother with a pawing child would immediately turn around and exit. But I continued to go in deeper, carefully making my way through the maze of *things*.

A large, rounded old man with glasses and short gray hair sat at a stool behind the counter. He was helping two women as I entered. He looked jolly, smiling at the women as he talked. He wore a simple, sky blue collared shirt that accentuated his blue eyes. A white beard with a red suit would make him a perfect candidate for Santa Claus.

He shot me a quick but kind look. I smiled back in acknowledgement and began looking around. I wasn't interested in buying anything, simply killing time. I was overwhelmed by all the stuff and questioned the sanity of anyone who would spend money on it. Then the old man paused from helping the ladies.

"Anything you want to know about anything in the store, just ask and I will tell you a story," he shouted happily in accented English to me. His words were light and airy and flowed together like the start of a musical melody.

"Thank you," I replied as I turned my head in his direction. I was skeptical of his genuineness and believed he simply wanted to make a sale.

The ladies left, leaving the old man and I alone. I picked up one of the statues.

"I've got a story for that," the old man spoke.

I smiled politely and placed the statue back down. I was determined not to buy anything but continued looking around. I picked up another statue still wondering who would purchase it and why.

"I've got a story for that as well," he playfully said again.

I didn't want to talk and was going to leave. But then something inside of me was curious and decided to nibble his offer like a fish on a worm. I figured it was a *conversation* I was looking for and an opportunity to hear some Greek stories. And I didn't have to buy anything.

Noticing what resembled a rosary of beads near the counter, I was curious what they were. Since I arrived in Greece I noticed many Greek men carrying them around. I picked one up.

"Ok, tell me the story behind these," I said to the old man.

"Ah, the komboloi beads are very special to the Greeks," he began.

"Komboloi?" I tried to understand what he said.

"Yes, worry beads," he continued. "In ancient Greece when the men traveled on sea between the many islands for battle, the water was sometimes very rough and there were many shipwrecks." His tone changed to a hush, adding drama like a seasoned storyteller. "The men would carry the komboloi with them and pass each bead through their fingers to help occupy and distract their minds from worrying and for serenity."

It was a nice story and I liked their purpose. So I bought one for my father and one for myself.

Next I noticed a statue of four monkeys that was vaguely familiar. One monkey covered his mouth, the next his ears, and the third his eyes. But I had never seen a fourth one, who covered his crotch. It reminded me of my mother's "four monkeys", as she playfully called my brothers and I as children. So I picked it up.

"What is the fourth one for?" I asked. "I've seen this image before with three but never a fourth."

"Ah," he began as a laugh came rising from his belly and a smile to his face. "See no evil, hear no evil, speak no evil, and do no evil." I laughed along with him then added it to my purchases as a gift for my mother.

"And these?" I said pointing through glass at circle medallions with colored rings of black, white and blue.

"Those are called evil eyes," he said. "They are to ward off evil spirits. You wear or hang them in your home for protection."

I liked the message and bought one each for Jim and Christy to protect the police officers in our family.

I began to enjoy the old man's company and continued picking up different pieces throughout the shop. With each item he relayed a story. And my family received more gifts. He spoke with pride and happiness as he expressed each tale. Over an hour passed as I time-traveled throughout mythological sagas of ancient Greece.

Remembering my attitude upon first entering the shop, I laughed to myself. Believing only crazy people would buy such items while I scanned the counter full of touristy *things* I was about to purchase. But I was tickled with my experience and had no regrets.

"You're a good salesman," I said with a smile, directing his attention to all the stuff between us.

"Ah, yes. It is how I make my living. But it is my passion meeting the people that come through the door. It brings me great joy to be able to share my stories and country with foreigners. It does not matter to me if you buy anything. I have enjoyed our time together."

"Thank you," I replied. "Me too."

"I am Dimitri," he said as he extended his hand. "With seven 'I's.'"

I looked at him confused as I quickly spelled Dimitri in my head and wondered how seven I's fit into his version.

"There are three eyes in my name and four more eyes here," he said, pointing to his own eyes and glasses. We shared a laugh. "I come from a family of four boys." My heart skipped at our connection.

"I come from a family of four boys as well," I said.

"Ah, but one of my brothers recently passed away," he said with new sadness. My eyes widened with amazement as our bond deepened.

"One of *my* brothers recently passed away too," I replied as the memory came rushing back.

He then, noticing my age and sorrow in my eyes, realized my brother must have been young. Immediately he switched his focus from his experience to my mother and I.

"Ah, if your mother is a woman of great faith, and you as well, you will find strength. And that everything will be all right," he said with compassion in his tone.

The gesture was tender and touched me.

"Thank you," I replied, "for *everything.*" I gathered my bags and began to leave.

"Thank *you,*" he said.

I left feeling lighter in my loneliness as Angel Dimitri played his part on my journey toward more peace inside over Joe's death and learning to live with it.

5

When I returned to Michigan I began working at a fine dining Italian restaurant called Noto's, owned by a family with Sicilian roots. They were strong believers in family and invited me into theirs. It became the perfect arrangement because when I needed to venture out and explore they let me go but I knew I always had a job waiting.

As the first winter holidays without Joe approached, I felt emotionally distanced from my family. I *wanted* to be there for them but didn't know how. It felt wrong to burden them with my grief because I knew they each carried a mountain of their own. But I also feared that their sorrow would make mine darker.

One afternoon I heard a distressing noise as I came down the stairs. It was my mother, alone, crying at the kitchen table. Of course I knew they were tears for Joe but I stood there frozen, listening to her sob, as my mind went blank with what to do. Such a simple act as going up and hugging her did not enter my mind. My emotional immune system was so fragile that I reacted as if her cries were a virus I could catch. I never realized we could lean on one another. Instead, each of us was left feeling we had to mourn and heal alone.

I continued down the stairs making enough noise that she would hear me and, as predicted she stopped crying and tried to compose herself. I intuitively understood she was trying to be strong for me. She resumed balancing her checkbook as if no tears had dropped. And I overflowed with misery and disappointment that I did not try to be strong for her.

But there were some moments of strength where I could separate myself from my pain and be supportive for one of my family members.

"I don't recall any memories of Joe," Jim said one day when we were sitting alone at the kitchen table. Jim was not someone to open up to me often about his feelings. I was caught off guard but the exposed vulnerability in his tone was like cold water splashed in my face. I concentrated on his every word.

"What do you mean?" I asked.

"I just can't get the image of him lying in the morgue out of my head," he continued. "The entire two hours Christy drove us to the hospital I chained-smoked and took shots of whisky wishing it was a mistake. I tried to convince myself one of Joe's friends borrowed his car."

"I am so sorry you had to be the one to do that," I said. "But you did a great service to our family, especially to Mom and Dad. Can you imagine if they were home when the police arrived and they had to go identify their own son? Not only would they have to live without Joe but seeing him like that would have twisted the knife deeper in their heart. It was best that they were unreachable. Your instincts were right to drive to the hospital first. Maybe it was a mistake. Mom and Dad would have been protected from even the thought."

"I didn't know they were an hour out of town at Justin's hockey game. I waited for them when I returned from school that day before we went to dinner. But if I had come home earlier, been there when the police came to the house, I wouldn't have believed them, or told anyone. I would have driven two hours to the hospital, alone, to prove the police wrong. Then kept the secret so nobody would ever have to hear such a terrible lie."

"But it was true. And if I was the one to identify Joe I would have gone a bit crazy. You were the strongest person to do it and luckily had Christy by your side. Thank you for that, and for saving me and the rest of our family from that image."

Jim's head was bowed. He slowly nodded, acknowledging my gratitude as the gravity of his sacrifice sunk in. It was a harsh push into adulthood.

"Do you have any memories of Joe and I," he asked timidly, as if holding on to a shear shred of hope for *something.*

"You know," I began, "when Joe first died all my childhood memories vanished. All I could associate with his name was death, funeral, casket and cemetery. But slowly as time went on I was flooded with many wonderful memories and moments. They'll come back to you. For me it is always 'Jim and Joe' together in February for your birthdays. I was always jealous that you two got to share your birthdays with one another."

"We were always jealous of you that you got to have your own party," he said.

"Really?" I said. "How funny. And we will always have Christmas. Even without specific memories, that extreme, pee-your-pants excitement and anticipation that we all shared together. *Those* are the childhood memories of siblings. Giving. Receiving. Playing together Christmas morning. It seemed the whole year built up to it. Remember going to Toys 'R' Us? Mom took us one by one around the store to choose Christmas gifts for the others while Dad waited with the rest of us. Then back at home we'd anxiously wait for them to be wrapped and put under the tree so we could shake them and try to guess what they were. I loved that."

"Yeah, me too," he said.

"And next year you and Christy will be married and I'm sure will soon have kids of your own to create similar memories, as well as new ones. Joe will come back to you, just believe."

The first Christmas Eve without Joe my family gathered at my uncle's. I went shopping with a friend beforehand, after which we stopped at a bar for a few drinks. It was a welcome distraction to share a few laughs before meeting up with my family. But once the alcohol kicked in, so did the painful dry ice burn of mourning Joe.

After taking my friend home, facing the holiday that was the cornerstone of childhood memories with one less brother was too overwhelming. I could not do it. I returned to the bar for a few more drinks, and never met up with my family. I felt more content alone, numbing the pain and filling the void with alcohol. Soon I was too drunk to drive but did anyway and fortunately safely made it back to an empty home.

Inside I listened to a CD of George Winston's piano playing. It was my Christmas present from Joe the previous year. I was sitting on the floor in the living room with only the lights of the Christmas tree reflecting off the ornaments.

About halfway through a track caught my attention. It was short and sweet, and had a very blithe spirit. It reminded me of Joe as I imagined him dancing along to it. I grabbed the CD case to find out the name. It was entitled "Graceful Ghost". I spoke aloud to Joe that whenever I heard it I would think of him, my Graceful Ghost. It would be our song.

I began to cry as the strength of the dry ice burn overpowered the dulling effects of the alcohol. Then I went upstairs to bed before my family returned. I couldn't imagine facing them in my state. All I wanted was to fast-forward through the night and rest of the year.

Christmas morning we went through the motions, all aware of the vast hole Joe's absence created. We did our best to be joyous when opening our gifts. But it simply seemed pointless and empty. I did not want to be there, but I could not comprehend being anywhere else *but there*. The fragileness in the air was terrifyingly palpable like a butterfly in the hands of a child, unaware of its delicacy.

The truth and finality was too crushingly close. We had walked, stumbled, and crawled through a marathon of firsts without Joe. But with Christmas the painful Year of Firsts was nearly over. As extended family arrived it became a tiny bit easier; the physical void filled with the energy of more people. Praising aunts, uncles and cousins kept Joe alive. With them around, we were able to hear his name and listen to others' memories. Perhaps even share one of our own. They helped sedate our sadness and gently nudged us through the day and into 1999, our second year of life.

After the New Year I traveled the west coast for a month. I began in Los Angeles, investigating it as a potential place to move and start an advertising career. I continued driving north along the coast, spending time in San Francisco, Bend, Oregon and ending in Seattle. Driving through flourishing beauty and abundance of nature aided the forward movement of my life. But after returning, I decided Los Angeles and the west coast in general was too far from my family. I chose Chicago instead which was only three hours from Grand Rapids.

I moved in mid-May, just after my birthday, and began looking for work. Wearing my high school graduation suit, I walked the streets of downtown Chicago and dropped my resume off at the major advertising agencies. But truth be told I did not have much motivation or passion to succeed. The paralysis of grief had followed me to Illinois.

Then a friend from Michigan State who worked at Foote, Cone and Belding arranged an interview for an entry-level position in account management. Once I completed the interview, I was given a tour of the floor where I would work. It was an expansive open space of monotonous cubicles stretching across the floor, row after row, with a few aisles in between. The sounds of telephones ringing and mumbles of conversations talking business provided the soundtrack. Only the top of an employee's head was visible in his workspace, resembling a worker bee in a fluorescent-lighted hive. It felt suffocating and flavorless.

A week later I received a call.

"This is Debra from Foote, Cone and Belding," she said. "We interviewed last week."

"Yes I remember," I said. "How are you?"

"Good thank you. I wanted to let you know we have a position available for you."

"OK," I said timidly.

"I'm doing some internal rearranging with my current employees. Just give me a call next week and I will have a clearer idea of which account I will place you on."

"Alright," I said. "Thank you." As soon as I hung up the reality hit. *Do I* really *want to be a pawn, working in a cubicle at a big agency and have my life be learning and knowing everything there is to know about macaroni and cheese or some other product?*

I never called her back.

It was time to search for something I felt passionate about doing but I had difficulty finding a starting point for the search. As the dry ice vault continued to change forms from solid into foggy vapor I was veiled and confused with grief. The days became long and lonely. As the record-breaking humidity of summer sizzled, I remained numb.

Additionally I found it arduous meeting new people. I was familiar from my traveling days with sharing intimate details about my life—minus the subjects of sex and love—very quickly. Sometimes with only an afternoon or a day with a person I felt the desire to express my thoughts and feelings on life based on my collective experiences. It was a way of rapid bonding that was often reciprocated, leading to a better understanding of each other. And it often provided new insight on life to absorb into my own.

So I used the same approach with people I met in Chicago. Naturally I spoke of Joe's death and the travels that evolved from it. Together they were my yin and yang, my happiness and sadness, my dark and light and the ends of my spectrum.

"Really?" some would say. "So what do you do for a living?"

In a sensitive and vulnerable state I felt they wanted to change the subject. I didn't think they cared to learn the Joe part of me. But it was still an enormous facet of my life and I needed to share it.

If I was not asked questions about Joe or his death then there was nothing to answer. If I had nothing to answer, I could not speak about Joe. If I could not speak about Joe in a new place or with new people not connected to him then it made it seem like he didn't exist anymore—that he was dead. And wouldn't carry on. At least in hearing myself speak of his life and death he was still with me.

"I'm a traveler," I would respond. I still identified myself with what I felt were exciting and unique experiences to share.

"So what are you doing in Chicago?" would inevitably be the next question.

"Well, I have a degree in advertising and I am looking for a job," I would reply insecurely. But it was a sensitive subject to me because I didn't have a job or any direction at the time. I was still prone to philosophical topics about life and death. I was not socially adept to a lighter approach in getting to know someone.

Internalizing what seemed to me as their lack of interest in my brother's death, I was hurt and took it very personally. A seed of self-hate and rage bloomed that would unfairly be projected on "them" for not wanting to get to know me. But it was really me that didn't want to get to know myself.

At the end of June I returned to Michigan for Jim and Christy's wedding. I took my old friend Daphne as my date. Daphne was born in Korea. When she was three her father went to Cairo to establish a missionary. But a year later he was killed in a car accident. Her mother then moved Daphne and her two older sisters to Cairo to continue his work.

Once Daphne and her sisters reached adolescence her mother sent them to be educated in Michigan under the guardianship of a friend living in Grand Rapids. She felt it would provide a better opportunity then what they could receive in Egypt. It was in Grand Rapids that I met Daphne while working as lifeguards at a water park. We learned we went to rival high schools and over the summer became good friends.

Daphne was short at 5'4" with long, straight black hair. She was a vision of purity, beauty and intelligence. She was gracious, kind and thoughtful. The type of woman any man would proudly introduce to his mother.

After high school we remained in touch throughout college. She was a studious free spirit who studied at the Sorbonne in Paris her first year and then in Jerusalem her second. We kept in touch with letters while she was overseas. Every time an envelope marked *PAR AVION* with the blue and red markings arrived in the mail I got a thrill knowing its point of origin was France, Israel, or sometimes Egypt if she was visiting her mother. For her remaining two years of college she transferred to the University of Michigan during the time I was at Michigan State.

Daphne was enviably international, cultured, and had traveled all around the world. I always imagined her to be the perfect woman for me. We could be silly, jumping in fountains like children one minute, before getting lost in deep conversations on life and beliefs for hours the next. But I never acted on it. The image of her as the fairytale woman to marry remained a One-Day fantasy in my head. My heart was increasingly certain of something else that left it impossible to make the fantasy real. But I tried to push Mars through Venus and Jim's wedding was another attempt.

I had invited Daphne to the wedding while we were together earlier that year in Chicago on the first anniversary of Joe's death. She was working in Egypt on a one-year internship planning a charity event for an American company to be held at the Pyramids for the Millennium celebration but returned to visit her sisters who were living in Chicago. She asked if I would attend the future party in Egypt. I wanted to invite her as my date to the wedding. So we made a pact.

"I can't believe you made it back from Cairo for the wedding," I said to her in the limo after the ceremony.

"I'm just glad it worked out that the company needed me back in America during this time and I could get away to come," she said. "Besides, we made a deal. Remember, if I came to the wedding you promised to come to Cairo for New Year's. So now it's your turn."

"I know," I said. "I just don't know if it will work out. I haven't found a job yet and when I do I don't know if they'll let a new hire have time off right away."

"Please come," she said. "I have always wanted to show you where I grew up and it will be an amazing celebration."

"I do want to," I said. "I promise I will try."

After the wedding I returned to Chicago. I prayed to Joe to help me discover my passion as he had discovered his in dance.

For the Fourth of July Dallas came to Chicago to visit. One evening Dallas and I, my two roommates—also former fraternity brothers—and a group of other Michigan State transplants went bar hopping. As the night progressed the group grew smaller. Eventually Dallas returned with my roommates to our place. I was in a self-destructive mood. Drink after drink, the night progressed. With each new bar the group began to shrink, until there was one. Me. Alone.

I wandered onto Haltsead Street in Boystown. It was the main street of the gay neighborhood lined with bars and clubs. I began to go into each one. I never stayed long enough to *stop* and have a drink or speak to someone. I just browsed the boys, absorbed the atmosphere of their world, and explored. I rarely made eye contact. If I did it was by accident or I was caught.

When the bars closed I paced Halstead while the streets emptied. But I wasn't ready to go home. Like a dog with an invisible fence around his home, as soon as I reached the border of the neighborhood I turned around. I yearned for more of an experience in *that* world. But I had no idea what that would involve. Even if I knew what I wanted to happen I didn't know how to communicate it. I was a foreigner who could not speak the local language.

While roaming I noticed an attractive Latin man standing at a bus stop. He was in his early twenties, 5'9" with black hair. Built with muscles, he filled out the tight, black tank top he wore with beige cargo shorts. We were the only people there.

As I approached I slowed down. I sneaked a look. Caught. He made eye contact and gave a slight smile. Not understanding we had just communicated, I carried on walking three more blocks. Then the "fence" alerted me to turn around, stay home. So I went back. As I came upon the boy, he was facing me. Again he smiled. I looked but carried on walking. After a few blocks I turned around, again, and as I passed he flashed me another a smile.

It felt like we were two actors shooting a night scene. Take after take I was screwing the scene up by not saying my lines. And the movie of my life would not continue in the way my heart desired until I did.

But gradually I began to feel more comfortable because we were alone on the street. It felt safer to interact. Along with the playful look in his eyes and warm smiles I felt invited into his world. So my confidence slowly grew. Finally after the fifth lap, circling like a lion, I took the first step into a new exploration by stopping.

"Hi," I said.

"Hi," he responded.

"Where are you going?" I asked.

"Home," he said.

Then a streak of courage ran through me. Born with an explorative gene I was always curious to try just about anything once. As temptation for an experience with another man flooded my body, the dam was ready to burst. It was time to make it tangible. Every moment remained unknown. But each one pushed the door open as my curiosity ached to know what was on the other side.

"Would you like some company?" I asked, speaking the language.

"Sure," he said with a smile as the bus approached. "It's quite a long ride to my house, about forty-five minutes."

"That's alright," were my words as we both boarded. But my nervousness peeked. I was terrified what to talk about for such a long ride. Or share any truths about my life. So I created a new identity and story for myself.

I was wearing a shirt that said, "Bend, Oregon", which I bought on my travels. I told him I lived there and was just visiting Chicago. It helped that I had been there so recently as I told him all about "life" in Oregon. It filled up the time and became effortless, as the tale took on a life of its own.

Dawn was near when we arrived at his home. I had no precise expectations in asking to come over, nor any clear-cut indication about his intentions or desires. I simply wanted continuation, in the company of a man. He gave me a quick tour, ending in his room. I needed a moment alone and asked to use the bathroom.

I stayed in there for several minutes, not knowing what to do. I found some toothpaste and used my finger as a brush. Instinct told me to freshen up my mouth. When I got out he was tidying up his room.

"Would you like something to drink?" he asked.

"Water, thanks," I quietly replied.

As he went to the kitchen, I sat down on the edge of the bed. He returned and stretched over the bed from the other side to hand me a glass.

"Here you go," he said.

"Thank you," I replied as I turned my body to face him, eyes on the glass, and grabbed the water. Our hands touched with the exchange.

I resumed facing forward, my back to him and took a sip. Then set the glass on the carpet. I turned again toward him with my head down and slowly looked up at him. He was now on the bed, lying on his side, one arm propping him up as his head rested in his hand. He left a respectable amount of space between us and smiled sweetly. I felt frozen and did not know what to do next. Sensing he was going to have to make the first move, he gently leaned in and began kissing me.

I closed my eyes and kissed back, sensually and slowly. I was still a bit drunk but the contact felt natural, as my lips sang *Hallelujah!* Parts of my body came to life after waiting for twenty-three years. My hands shouted, *Let us play!* And so one went to his cheek while the other ran gradually up his arm. His skin was soft to touch. His supple muscles welcomed my squeeze. Then my curious fingers rose to the back of his head and ran through his coarse black hair.

Things quickly turned more passionate as I gave in to it. My hands slid down his back then grasped his shirt from the sides and pulled it up. As I did, his arms raised to assist me. Then he reached for and began to lift my shirt. I crossed my arms over my body touching his hands. As I did he removed his then leisurely lied on his back and put his arms behind his head to take in my debut moment.

I unzipped his shorts and pulled them down, discovering he preferred neither boxers nor briefs. There lying in front of me was a gorgeous, naked young man and *I* was in bed with him. I paused for a moment staring at his nude body.

It was magnificently masculine; his V-shaped torso, the hair underneath his arms and on his legs. His cock was growing with every moment and with a life of its own. Inching up, *several* inches toward his navel, as he patiently waited for me, unaware of his relaxed and sexy pose. It was the body of a man but he had the excitement of a boy in his eyes, eager to play with another boy. And as he became aroused, beneath my shorts another life rose and shouted, *My turn!*

I pressed my body on top of his as all the years of desire began to emerge, like Penelope reuniting with Odysseus. Only the two living and breathing bodies existed. Nothing else was felt, not even the bed on which we lied. As the mind and all of its ingrained doctrines was muzzled. We were simply two warm bodies inhaling and exhaling, focusing every ounce of attention and energy on the other. My heart's pace increased.

But with excitement, its twin nervousness accompanied. As I dove deeper into the experience there were instances of pulling back. My mind's muzzle squirmed to escape. Like a time traveler caught in a portal, a foot in the past and one in the future, it disconnected me from the realm I was trying to break into. I tried to become in sync with his energy, focusing on how to pleasure him. Then he gently took the reins, hungry to discover what I wanted and to pleasure me. I stopped.

"I've never really done this," I finally said to him.

"What?" he asked.

"Been with a man," I said.

He was intoxicated as well and just smiled endearingly. With that truth out of me, I was freed to surrender deeper to the moment. It connected me to him, because now he knew that he was my first, Numero Uno. And the hopeful wishes for at least a decent experience that came with it, unlike with Jockey or the Key West Queens, who were still completely blocked from my memory. In my eyes I was a virgin because Uno was my first man that I was conscious for and, with my deliverance, passion ensued as we resumed kissing and touring each other's body.

We rolled with him on top of me. Uno began pleasuring my body; running his hand down my chest, squeezing my pectoral, gently pinching and playing with my nipple. Then brushing his hand over my stomach, pausing as his hand rose with my breath. Next the hand continued down, unbuttoned and pulled my shorts down to end Its hibernation. Then grabbed ahold and took It into his warm mouth.

I felt safe in Uno's bed. Nobody I knew had any clue where I was or what I was doing. It helped to make me fully present to explore the naked man next to me.

Like a racehorse straight out of the gate I was eager to explore *everything* about being with a man. Soon I went down on Uno and took pleasure in smelling the remains of a faint scent of showered cleanliness combined with the manly sweat from a night of dancing. It made me even more excited. And I wanted more. I began desiring to be inside him. To feel what that was like. So I came up to meet his eyes.

"Do you want me to fuck you?" I asked shyly.

Uno simply reached for a condom from his nightstand. Then took me in his mouth again before placing it on. He straddled me and guided me into him. I just lied there and watched. He closed his eyes while his body adapted to me inside. Then slowly started moving up and down. I released all control to Uno. It turned me on even more to watch him on top of me, connected in that way. I could not take my eyes off him. I wanted to be closer. So I sat up and began kissing him.

We then turned over and I began sliding in and out. It felt warm, comfortable as our body heat combined and intensified. I was going moment to moment, not really comprehending what I was doing, allowing Uno to guide me.

But at the same time, my body and its pieces, all part of the action, and with the excitement of a pep rally, did what they wanted and had desired for over ten years. Not holding back on anything. It felt liberating. I nestled into Uno like I was with my own kind after what seemed like lifetimes away on another planet. And although I was fighting off the drunken feelings, still I was ravenous for more.

"Do you want to fuck me?" I then asked.

I lay there on my back as I watched him, kneeling over me, while placing the condom on. He never lost eye contact with me. The curiosity of what it would be like raced through my head and out my eyes. Slowly Uno went in. I tried to relax as he continued to push further in. It hurt. His hips began to pull back before moving in again, back and forth. I could not take too much before I placed my hand on his abdomen to gently push him out. I was too shy to speak after such an intimate moment.

"Try getting on top of me," Uno softly said.

He lied on his back. I straddled him and guided him back in me. Up and down I slowly started to move. But after a few moments it was still too uncomfortable. I took him out and rolled the condom off.

I felt insecure and timid exploring so much with a man right away. But at the same time, in his drunken state, I didn't feel he cared much what we did. Uno was gentle with me, allowing me to go at my own pace and try what I wanted.

Next I began to perform oral sex on him. But soon I heard a soft snore. Uno had passed out. I tried to wake him ready to continue but he was out for the night. Even asleep his naked body aroused me. So I sat on top of him and masturbated, climaxing all over his chest.

I then lied next to him for a moment. Until the reality of what I had done struck like lightning and I bolted out of bed. I grabbed a towel to wipe his chest, got dressed and left. It was early morning and daylight had come. I hailed a cab, rushed back into the city and into my own bed. I woke in the early afternoon. Dallas was already up.

"Where did you go last night?" he asked.

"I just went to a few bars after you left. Then I came home," I said.

"Did you have fun?"

"Ehh, typical night," I lied. "Too much drinking and now paying for it."

"Let's go eat. I've got a craving for Chicago deep dish," he said. "That should help your hangover."

While at lunch I wanted to escape my body and flee from being around my old friend but feared it would look suspicious. It felt as if I was suffocating and I dreaded him probing for any more details about the night. I would lie, but I didn't want to be put in that position.

Somehow I felt he already could see right through me. I put on the best performance I could muster up, acting like the Jason he knew. All the while inside my mind was racing, as bombs of fear and anxiety continually exploded. In the reality of day, remembering what Uno and I did absolutely terrified me—the memory eating me alive.

Part of it had to do with the ingrained Catholicism that judged it was wrong. The other part was my own feeling that *I* did not want to be gay. I still held the dream of marriage with a woman, with Daphne.

As the holiday ended I became obsessed with figuring out how to escape from the experience with Uno and myself. The only solution I could fathom was leaving Chicago. If I moved, the person I was beginning to be and the experience with Uno would remain here. So I turned once again to traveling, the answer to my passion and my escape.

The escape of moving or taking a trip did have a positive effect. It gave inspiration to keep living because I still felt passion in discovering new places. But it also bought me time and provided breathing room from dealing with a crushing amount of emotions. Whenever I moved or traveled my mind was occupied. I had to learn my way around and get settled.

I began to research the possible career options in the travel industry. During the process I interviewed for a temporary job doing promotions for a company that marketed products to college students. The fact that I would be sent *somewhere* to a college—providing an escape for a moment—attracted me to the position.

I received the job but instead of being sent to a new destination, they sent me to a college in Michigan, forty minutes from where I grew up. I took it as a sign to move back to Grand Rapids, regroup, and further explore the possibility of a career in travel. Moving back with my family also allowed me to save money and keep my promise to Daphne. I could slip into the old Jason and try to forget Uno and Chicago. And as I boomeranged back, Noto's happily welcomed me with a job.

After a month in Michigan I found in the paper a course to be trained as a travel agent. It began just as my temporary job ended. I signed up and went to school during the day while waiting tables at night.

A few weeks after the promotions assignment concluded the company contacted me. The campaign I worked on was a huge success and the company surprised a group of the promoters with a weekend vacation as a bonus. To Key West, it called me back.

It was in Key West that I again had two drunken nights that led to two more one-night stands with men. It was safer, in my sober state once I left, because it was easier to leave those experiences behind. No one would have to know. And I kept telling myself it could *never* happen again as I prepared to go to Egypt.

6

I landed in Cairo around 4 a.m. on the last day of the millennium. Once through customs a man approached me offering a cab ride into the city. In my jet-lagged intoxication I simply nodded. He led me to a car where another man waited in the driver's seat. I entered the back—handing him a card with the Windsor Hotel's address as he took the passenger seat. Off we sped away. *Fast.*

I was soon surprised at how crowded the main highway was with cars at such an early hour. And they were all going just as fast, each beeping their horns and flashing their blinkers like Morse code to one another. My driver kept weaving in and out of lanes passing cars while performing his own blinks and honks. Both men upfront talked to each other nonchalantly while I swayed heavily from side to side in the back.

Initially there were moments of concern for my safety. But as I watched the other cars drive in the same manner, I trusted they knew what they were doing.

It was an unexpected first impression of Egypt; the middle of the night, chaotic ride with lights, noise and traffic. Not that I assumed the plane would land in the desert amongst the pyramids. I simply never would have foreseen such activity. It woke me up.

But by the time I checked in to the hotel and my head reached the pillow, I fell into a deep sleep to be ready for the dream to continue when

I woke. Which it did with the rattling sound of an old-fashioned bell ring of the phone next to my bed and ear.

"Hello?" I sleepily said.

"Good morning! Welcome to Egypt!" It was Daphne. "Did I wake you?"

"Yes, but it's okay," I said. "Thank you for the wake-up call. I should get up anyway. Would you like to meet somewhere?"

"I have last minute preparations for the party to attend to," she said. "I won't be able to see you until tonight. I'm sorry. But there is a nice open market you can check out near your hotel. Is there anything *you* want to do?"

"That's alright, I understand. I'll just go for a walk and get a feel with the area," I said.

She instructed me where to meet her that night. Then I headed out into exotic *Egypt*. It still seemed unreal. It was my first time in a third world country and being a minority. I began to wander and came upon a market—I assumed it was the one Daphne mentioned. There were hundreds of people buying and selling everything from bras to pens to all kinds of food. Butchers had three to four whole cattle skinned and hung in front of the shops as flies swarmed around.

Without any other Caucasian men or women present, I received many looks from people. It made me feel bashful and exposed. I pulled the hood of my black jumper over my head to blend in and block the midday sun.

Egyptian children were some of the most stunning I had ever seen. They had a natural and exotic bohemian essence with their curly black hair and dark complexions. The dust from the streets would gently blanket their bodies and clothes from head to bare feet but they wore it beautifully, naturally, and with pride like the land and earth they came from. Their large eyes would bulge in wonderment when I made eye contact. It made me feel like a movie star. Some gave the impression I was the first white man they had ever seen.

"Hi! Hi! Welcome! Welcome!" some would shout and repeat in English like a scratched record when they saw me.

I wandered in to the middle of the market, shoulder to shoulder within a sea of Egyptians. It was not for anyone with a fear of crowds. There was a microcosm of hundreds of people going about their day getting what they needed for their individual lives. But at the same time the macrocosm of a culture 7000 years old felt strong, alive, and working.

Suddenly I felt a hand placed between my shoulder blades. A woman in a burka had noticed I was going through the crowd in the direction she desired and gently pushed and guided us through. It felt exhilarating as the adrenaline rushed through me like I had truly made *contact* with the people and culture. As if from that moment the dream had turned from black and white into color.

Throughout many of the streets and alleys people knelt down on carpets with their bellies to the ground, arms stretched out in front of them to pray. The city's large Muslim population introduced to me up-close the rituals of Islam. I was fortunate to be there during the holy holiday of Ramadan. Five times throughout the day the Muslims are required to pray. It felt ingrained in the people's day much like going to the market or post office. Sometimes an Imam led the people in prayer while other times people privately knelt down and got up on their own accord. It was a beautifully somber and spiritual experience.

Car horns and traffic noise intertwined with the Arabic spoken throughout the market along with chants of prayer. Together it produced a symphony of sounds that was both a busy and peaceful hum of life to my ears.

I did not speak much aside from "hello" and "thank you" to the children welcoming me. At times I felt very timid. I hoped to give the utmost respect to the people and culture as I snapped pictures of the architecture. But my lens always seemed to be magnetically drawn to the people. I tried to capture candid shots of what seemed to me like exotic individuals doing ordinary things; a man in a turquoise sweater and denim who seemed to be standing on the sea of people, shouting to the crowd what he had to sell and for how much and a beautiful boy about four-years-old who hitched a ride on his father's shoulders through the masses. The child connected me to my father and the fond memory of doing the same. Snap. Snap. I quickly pushed the camera's shutter button then pulled my camera down, hoping that I did not offend anyone.

After exiting the market I made my way down a more central road. I continued walking the opposite direction from my hotel until I stopped at a bridge that stretched over a body of water that needed no introduction. For I knew, it was the Nile.

Across the Nile the city was more modern and western world friendly. Hotels lined the banks of the river and separated the poorer, more local area I ventured from and called home for my visit. But I felt tucked more deeply into the country as a local on my side.

Hotels and modernism aside, I stood there for a moment and took in the famous river whose name stretched a continent and time. Its calm and simple current flowed like a vein, giving movement to life and life to an old city. I felt connected to history. The Nile was like an immortal ancestor I heard legends about all my life that I was meeting for the first time. And I felt welcome.

I decided to return to my hotel. On the way I walked on the opposite side of the main road, which was quieter and with less people. I came upon a small side street that I was curious to explore and turned right off the main road. The first pathway in that ran parallel to the main road I turned left to continue toward my hotel.

The alleyway was much narrower and darker from the shadows cast by the closely packed buildings. There were mainly men slowly wandering about as I made my way through. Some stood while others sat in the doorways of different buildings no more that a few stories high on each side. They all took long, lingering looks at me as I passed. I kept my focus straight ahead of me on the path, only glancing slightly from side to side. There were only a few feet on each side of me to the buildings. A tension filled the air. I intuitively decided to be extra-cautious and limit any movement, even breathing too deeply, beyond walking. I took the first left I could that led back to the main road.

Not long after I exited I noticed an Egyptian man of my similar age walking directly behind me. He gradually closed the gap between us. I kept moving and remained looking forward. Then he was beside me. I braced myself and carefully looked toward him to see what he may do.

"Where are you from?" he asked as we both continued walking, my guard still up.

"America," I said.

"And what are you doing in Egypt?" he said.

"Visiting a friend." I kept my answers short, remaining cautious.

"And what were you doing back there?" he continued.

"Just exploring the city a bit," I replied. He started to smile and attempted to hold back a chuckle.

"Why do you ask?" I said.

"Well, it is just that you should not go to that area if you do not need to," he said smiling warmly. "It is where you go to get drugs, and other things and . . . well it is not a very safe place for a foreigner to go."

"Really?" I asked quite surprised and relieved that nothing happened.

"How long have you been here?" he asked.

"I just arrived this morning," I replied, to which he began laughing.

"And already you have discovered the not-so-nice area," he said through laughter. His demeanor now put me at ease and I started laughing at my Curious George like act.

"I noticed you go in there and I followed behind," he continued. "I wanted to make sure nothing happened to you."

"Really? Thank you," I said, touched by the gesture.

"It is my pleasure. I would like you to leave safely and live to tell of it," he said. "What are you doing while here?"

"My friend helped plan a party at the pyramids tonight," I said. "I'm going to get ready now."

"Ahhh, that will be nice," he said. "I will be there too, down in front with all of the Egyptians. Well I hope that you and your friend have a wonderful time. And a happy new millennium."

"Insha'Allah," I replied. "And you too." His eyes got big.

"Ahh you know Arabic?" he asked smiling.

"Just that. My friend always says it," I said. "And 'habibi.'" He smiled more.

"Well then enjoy my country. And be safe, insha'Allah, habibi," he stated.

"Yes, 'god willing, my beloved,'" I translated back to him. "And thanks again."

"You are welcome my American friend," he said as he turned to cross the street, waving his hand high.

Once I arrived to my hotel I showered and prepared for the party. I put on my tuxedo and felt the extreme end of the spectrum after experiencing the poverty of the people and city throughout the day. As I stood there in my crumbling hotel room—whose grandeur had faded but its character remained from the baths for the Egyptian royal family it had been built to be at the turn of the last century—I felt like I had been transported through a gateway from a Hollywood premiere into a different time.

The contrast of class would be even more evident as soon as I left my room. On the outside and in their country I was extreme upper class. But inside and in my country I was financially poor, by American standards, and part of its lower class. Still I felt more connected to the Egyptians, especially from the events of the day. It was a Cinderella moment.

I met Daphne and her family in a beautiful and grand lobby at another hotel. Buses lined the entrance to transport hundreds of people into Giza where the Pyramids awaited our arrival. My excitement exponentially escalated imagining what it would be like to see the pyramids live, after twenty years of seeing pictures in books and in movies.

Our full bus left the lights of the city behind as the darkness grew and the stars multiplied. Our caravan slowly and carefully moved along as a swarm of thousands made their way toward the edge of the desert where the pyramids stood not far beyond. I was facing forward, sitting in an aisle seat on the right near the back. Suddenly a woman toward the front on my left shouted.

"There they are! The pyramids! I can see them!"

Everyone turned their bodies and looked to the left side of the bus, taking up much of the window space. I attempted to stand at my seat and peek through a small space between two heads. I gazed far into the distance for any sign of three black, silhouette triangles against the midnight blue star lit sky.

But I did not see anything and I became anxious, especially when I heard the "Wows" from the people that did. I shifted my position. This time when I looked back out the window I noticed a large dark space in front of me. When I readjusted my focus on the forefront rather than the distance I saw two dramatic diagonal lines that separated the lighter sky from the darker space. They stretched up toward each other and met somewhere above the bus. That is when I realized it was a pyramid and we were riding right past it. My jaw dropped. It was a powerful way to make an entrance and flushed me with excitement.

It felt like playing hide-and-go-seek in the dark as a child. The pyramid acting like a hidden parent I'm trying to find. I couldn't have imagined a better way to experience it for the first time.

Then I spotted another one.

We drove past them to a plateau where many different tents were erected, each hosting their own celebration. Beneath our tent resembled a grand dining room to match the likes of any five-star hotel complete with chandeliers. Around fifteen to twenty large round tables filled the room and sat ten. They were all set with the proper cutlery, china and glassware for a seven-course dinner. Some items on the menu included goose liver with plum and apricot compote, quail consommé with dumplings filled with quail meat, sautéed veal on a velvety red wine sauce, Sarladaise potatoes flavored with truffles, extra bitter chocolate cake, sweet delights, and more. I met some other Americans from all walks of life but people from countries around the world filled the tents. I took in the experience primarily with Daphne's sisters while she buzzed around mingling and being congratulated for creating the red carpet styled event. Jubilation and activity filled the air as the staff quickly tried to keep to the schedule. There was so much to take in of the surreal fairytale oasis that time accelerated with a humming vibration.

A wooden balcony was built to overlook the pyramids, the backdrop of the event. With the animation of children who could not sit still or even cared about the meal we escaped to the balcony in between courses, our minds racing and wondering when and how the celebration would start.

Down below from the plateau a stage was built in front of the pyramids. Front and center, and rightfully so, thousands of Egyptians stood in the desert. Suddenly as we were on course three or four the majestic sound of chimes being struck one by one signaled the commencement. We all rushed to the balcony.

From there we watched as French composer Jean-Michele Jarre debuted an original electro-orchestra entitled "12 Dreams of the Sun". It was performed to an explosion of fireworks and a rainbow of lights illuminating the pyramids from behind, welcoming the Millennium. The same pyramids that had played hide-and-seek were now rock stars shining on stage. And similarly to the unexpected cab ride and first impression into the city less than twenty-four hours earlier, my first taste of the pyramids surpassed all the pictures and movies. I felt as if I was hallucinating. As if the pyramids proudly said with a wink, "Hear we are, still standing after thousands of years. Not bad for a few old folks." Then just as quickly as it began it seemed to end. It was the year 2000. All the fears of terrorist attacks and Y2K seemed to blow away with the smoke of the final fireworks.

After the event Daphne ushered me through the crowds of people to one of the waiting buses and sent me off safely back to a hotel with some of the other attendees. She and her family, exhausted from all the stimulating activity, retired for the night. I didn't know where I was but continued to celebrate with champagne into the early hours of the morning. We then took a taxi back to the Marriott on the Nile where some of the more affluent guests were staying. Some wanted to continue the party but by then the ball had ended for me. Cinderella needed her beauty sleep. So I made my exit to my humbler hotel that I preferred for its ample charm.

From my walk during the day I was familiar with the area. I knew once I crossed over the Nile my hotel was roughly a mile away. A straight shot on the main road before taking a side street that curved like a question mark to my hotel. I thought the walk would be a nice way to take in the first hours of 2000 while sobering up with some fresh air as the sun rose.

Immediately after I was out-of-sight of the main road a car pulled up to me. There were two Egyptian men inside. Both were very slender and non-threatening in appearance. The man in the passenger seat had a moustache.

"Police! Police!" Moustache shouted in an Arabic accent as he quickly flashed some sort of identification.

I looked to see if I was the one being spoken to as the car stopped.

"Passport! Passport!" he began to shout.

The cocktail of even being in Egypt, the party, the pyramids, jet-lag, champagne, and being awake all day and all night produced a very dizzying state. I felt shaken like a martini.

I pulled out my travel security wallet hanging around my neck beneath my tuxedo shirt with all traces of my identity and every means of financial sustenance inside: my passport, two credit cards, $200 worth of Egyptian Pounds, $100 in traveler's checks and $50 American cash. Moustache snatched it and told me to get into the back of the car as he opened the door behind him. I entered without a thought. He had my life in his hands and every clue to me. I felt pulled to my passport but in the bizarre state, fear did not enter my mind. I sensed everything would be all right because the situation felt so unreal. I was more curious moment to moment what would happen next.

Moustache then reached in my wallet, pulled out the wad of Egyptian Pounds and handed them to me. I didn't think twice to quickly grab and put the wad in the breast pocket of my tuxedo. He went through the wallet so feverishly that I didn't think he realized he just gave up some of the cash. It felt like a movie where Bond, Jason Bond, gets kidnapped.

"Egyptian Pounds! Egyptian Pounds!" Moustache shouted as he turned around to look at me.

You just gave me the Egyptain Pounds, I thought. Confused and realizing what a predicament I was in, I tried to figure out how to get my wallet back.

"Let me show you, let me show you," I said, attempting to use a calm approach as I reached for the wallet to show him. I was hoping that way I could grab it and jump out the door. But he kept pulling the wallet away and shouting in Arabic.

The driver stayed quiet as if Moustache was in charge of the operation to steal the identity of Bond. He appeared apprehensive; his eyes screaming for Moustache to *complete his task* so he could do his and drive off.

"Out, out!" Moustache finally said as he rolled down his window. He then reached his hand out and opened my door from the outside. I was locked in and hadn't even known it. So I jumped out while my wallet remained hostage.

"Egyptian Pounds! Egyptian Pounds!" Moustache kept yelling.

I approached his window, trying to show him where in the wallet, but he continued to pull it away. Finally he reached his hand in, taking some of the contents out, and then threw the wallet to the ground behind me. I quickly turned around to seize it while the car sped off. Then I yelled a bushel of words that if my mother were near she would have inserted a bar of soap into my mouth to wash it out. And that was how the first morning of the new millennium started.

When I checked the travel wallet my passport and one credit card remained inside. The thieves stole the other credit card, the traveler's checks, and the $50 American dollars. But I was safe. And I was beyond exhaustion, entering a delirious state. I just wanted to sleep. But I knew I had to take care of what was stolen before I could.

The man at the front desk of my hotel had a 1920's operator phone system where he manually plugged in and out for each connection. It lacked the technology to make international calls. He directed me around the corner to a place I could call America. The Egyptian bills were too large for the small operation and I only had enough change to call for a few moments. My father answered the phone. It had just turned midnight in Michigan and they were celebrating with a group of friends.

"Dad, it's Jason," I began. I had not spoken to them since arriving in Egypt.

"It's Jason!" he excitedly said to the group. Their enthusiasm erupted and caused much noise as they all shouted "Happy New Year" to me.

"Dad! Dad!" I spoke louder, trying to get his attention.

"How is Egypt? How was the party?" he eagerly asked.

"Dad I got robbed. Cancel my MasterCard and the—"

"What? You got robbed?" His tone changed to concern. The group heard his words and with commotion they began asking what happened, drowning out my ability to continue.

"I'm fine! I'm fine!" I shouted grumpier by the second from the lack of sleep. "Dad please, I don't have much time left for this call. Just listen!" The man behind the counter held up both hands and began counting down the seconds with each finger. "Please just cancel my MasterCard and traveler's checks. I'm fine! *Just cancel* the MasterCard and traveler's checks," I got out just as the last finger went down and the connection was lost.

The robbery was history to me. I accomplished what I needed to take care of and *just wanted to sleep!* I was never happier to greet my bed.

Four hours later my phone rattled its bell loud into my ear.

"Hello?" I said half dead to the world. My body felt like it contained the weight of an immense boulder and I barely had the strength to move.

"Jason!" Daphne's voice came through with worry. "Are you alright? Your father called me and said you were robbed. What happened?"

"Daphne. I'm fine. I just need to sleep. I wasn't hurt. They didn't get away with much. I've taken care of it and now I simply need to sleep," I said.

"Are you sure?" she asked.

"Yes. Please. A little rest and I'll be good as new," I said reassuringly.

"Well my family and I want you to come out to eat with us tonight," she said.

"Yes, fine, that sounds nice," I responded.

"Great we'll be outside your hotel at 6:30," she said. "Take care of yourself and get some sleep."

"Ok, ok, bye," I said as I hung up the phone, my eyes already closed.

That evening we dined at a Korean restaurant in downtown Cairo. We ate with a group of Korean Ambassadors and dignitaries to Egypt that Daphne's mother knew through her missionary work. I was still exhausted from the entire preceding experience. Everyone at the table busily talked with each other in Korean. Daphne leaned in toward me to translate.

"They're saying how shocked they all are that you were robbed."

"It's really alright," I said. "It's over with."

"They're surprised," she continued. "They don't hear of that happening very often."

Daphne rejoined the Korean conversation while I was left in a realm of my own. I began contemplating the previous two days, trying to wrap my mind around where I was and what had happened—both positive and negative. But I still could not believe that Jason Anthony, a boy from Michigan, was the main character in the story being spoken of by strangers in Korean in ancient Cairo. I was feeling so far removed, out of my body, from everything and everyone at the table.

As I sat there my attention turned from the Korean conversation to the background music. Something felt familiar and my heart skipped a beat. I tuned my ears carefully to make sure. I was positive. "Graceful Ghost" was dancing and playing through the air. I smiled to myself and felt consoled.

That evening Daphne and I made arrangements to meet the next afternoon after I toured the Egyptian Museum to return to Giza. She hired a guide to take us on horses into the desert. I hoped as well to see the pyramids in the daylight without the fanfare of lights and fireworks.

As we entered the desert I could not determine where they stood. All I saw was the stretching sand. But as our horses gallantly ascended the hills of sand, Khufu, Khafre and Menkaura majestically appeared like the rising sun. The exact picture I had seen all my life in books and movies was right before my eyes. Only now, other senses that could not come from pictures added to my sight; the warmth of the sun on my body, the whistling wind as it broke around me, carrying the ageless grains of sand with it. I felt tranquility inside as the great pyramids grandly stood still before me.

I lowered myself from my horse and sat on one of the hills to quietly absorb the moment. The pyramids possessed a magnificent presence, and it seemed as if they were not only captivating me, but commanding me to simply spend time with them. I felt as though I were visiting a wise, elderly person, the two of us rocking together without words on a front porch. I felt peaceful and star struck. Not even the breeze blowing the sand into my eyes could ruin the communion we had—one of simply existing. Together. I began yearning to meet them up close. But alas, as our time came to a close, in the distance they remained.

As we entered a cab, and with one day left in Egypt, I wished that this would not be the last time the pyramids and I would be together. The taxi dropped us off at a restaurant for a late lunch, where Daphne introduced me to local foods such as baba ganoush, hummus, grape leaves, and falafel.

Ever since I arrived in Cairo Daphne seemed a little distant. I understood she steadfastly worked for twelve months on the event and was dedicated to giving 100 percent. It was one of the qualities I admired about her. I also knew that her work was mentally and emotionally draining, as she continually shared throughout the experience and my visit. And with the one night that had taken a year to plan now over, marking the conclusion of her internship, she was at a crossroads in life. I too was unclear about a direction beyond Michigan and the travel school. Luckily I had a seven-month internship at a travel company arranged to begin after I returned from Egypt. But after that I had absolutely no idea where life would take me.

Throughout lunch we spoke as usual with long and in-depth conversations about life and the places we still wished to travel. But toward the end there was an undertone of a slightly more intense direction initiated by Daphne.

"There is so much injustice in the world Jason. I want to help those without equality and basic human rights," she said with passion. "I admire my mother so much and the work that she does for women and children in this country and hope to make a difference like she has."

"I have no doubt that you will," I said, always knowing her to be a champion for world peace, especially in the Middle East. "If anybody can it's you. Your drive and ambition has always been inspiring to me. Your stories of travel led me out of Michigan to experience the world. And now you have brought me here."

She smiled slightly, expressing appreciation before continuing.

"I've put so much into this year and now it is time to move forward in a new direction. There is just so much I want to accomplish. I want to go to law school. But living back home in Egypt, having my mother near has been so wonderful too that I could see myself coming back here. And there are still so many places to travel," she said.

It seemed her words were building like a speech toward something important. So I chose to remain quiet. Be a friend and simply listen.

"I just don't see myself ever getting married and settling down," she finally stated then stopped, looking to me for a reaction. There was a pause. I didn't know if her speech was complete.

"Okay. You don't have to, if you don't want to," I said. "You will be a success at whatever you choose to do. Whether you create a family or world peace."

"Thanks Jason," she said as she put her head down.

It felt as if The Talk ended and she had expressed what she wanted. She suddenly appeared anxious and vulnerable looking around for the waiter.

"We should get going," she continued. "I have to get back to my family and you should experience the bazaar here. You can buy your family some gifts." We paid then walked outside. She hailed me a cab.

"So you leave tomorrow night?" she said as we stood at the rear entrance of the taxi.

"Not until four in the morning, so I have the whole day," I replied.

"Well I probably won't have a chance to see you again," she said. "I have some things to do tomorrow."

"That's okay. I understand. We'll talk soon," I said. "Thank you for everything. I'm really happy I came."

"I am too," she said. "Thank you for keeping your promise." We hugged and I entered the cab. She approached the passenger window and leaned in toward the driver. "Khan El Khalili," she said then stepped back and waved as we pulled out.

I turned toward the rear window for one last look and wave. When I did, a feeling struck. I felt like I had been dumped. I said to myself it was silly. I questioned how I could feel dumped when she was never my girlfriend. But regardless, to my surprise and confusion, dumped and empty in my heart is what I felt.

While at the bazaar I stumbled into the local part rather than the tourist area. An Egyptian man befriended me and took me around to all of his friends' workshops to see how and where many of the items were made. I bought common gifts seen in Cairo such as mother-of-pearl encrusted wooden boxes, delicate blown glass perfume bottles and scented oils for my family.

I was grateful for the unique experience and tour from the local. I felt a bit lonely since leaving Daphne and was happy to buy from his craftsman friends. Shopping therapy. They also sold it to me at a discount from what I would pay at the tourist area. And gave me lessons on bargaining for prices, encouraging me to do it as part of the culture.

He also brought me to a spice shop and showed me many different spices. I wasn't interested in buying anything else. But then he pulled out a tiny, blue plastic cylinder not taller than an inch with a green plastic top.

"This is a love spice," he said very mystically.

I looked at him confused as he took off the top. Inside was a substance that looked like lip balm.

"A love spice?" I repeated back to him to make sure I heard him correctly.

"Yes. You take just a little like this," he said as he scraped his pinky across the top a couple of times. "Then you rub it on the tip of your tongue." He demonstrated. "Then drink something very hot after and you will go for hours. Like rabbits." He moved his hips suggestively back and forth.

"Really?" I asked laughing.

"Yes. Love spice," he repeated.

"How much?" I asked his friend who was near.

"Fifteen Pounds," he said.

"How about ten," I said playfully getting into the bargaining.

"Twelve," he said smiling.

"Eleven," I came back.

"Sold!" he said with a big smile adding to my laugh about bargaining over pennies. So I returned to my hotel with no one to use the love spice on and went to sleep. But my view of the culture began changing after the experience of the robbery.

As I entered my last day my money was running out. The reality of the theft had caused some difficulty in getting my traveler's checks reimbursed. Because of Ramadan, unbeknownst to me, places closed early. And for some reason that was not revealed my remaining credit card company denied me a cash advance at each place I tried.

But by mid-afternoon of the last day I was able to get the $100 traveler's checks repaid in Egyptian pounds. I still had not seen the pyramids up close and was desperate to do anything to get another look. So I took a cab back to Giza for one last date.

Once there I hired a private guide to take me into the desert by camels. It was expensive to go on my own, but the guide took credit cards and the price wasn't a huge concern. It was my last day and I *had* to see the pyramids again.

I noticed he ran credit cards the old-fashioned way with carbon paper and an imprint of the card. I figured it would buy me some time in addition to the tour to sort out the situation in order to make sure he received payment, allowing me to save my cash to get out of Egypt.

As we entered the desert I noticed police riding around on camels. My guide approached one of the officers. They began speaking Arabic. Then my guide pulled out a few Egyptian pounds and handed it to him. The policeman accepted it and we went around to the other side of the pharaoh Khafre's pyramid in the center of the three.

"Go," he said. "You may climb up a bit."

"Really?" I asked not believing the unexpected words I heard.

"Yes just be careful," he replied.

As I climbed off my camel and approached the pyramid I felt minuscule compared to the glorious structure that rose above me. It was much different up-close from what I imagined. The smoothed limestone covering had been worn with the wind of thousands of years creating and revealing the building blocks effect. The large blocks were about two feet high and rose just above my knees.

I felt like the child in Shel Silverstein's *The Giving Tree* as I climbed each block. The pyramid was my tree and gave freely of itself, allowing me to climb upon and play. Whatever made me happy.

With each step that I took and every time I placed my hands on the next block to push up, I repeated to myself, *I'm climbing a pyramid, I'm climbing a* pyramid! in utter disbelief. But the sand and dust on my palms and between my fingers upon each block made it clearly evident. Along with the sun brightly shining down causing sweat to drip. I was indeed climbing a pyramid. And it was just the two of us.

I climbed roughly ten stories up then sat on one of the blocks. I turned to look at my guide. He seemed far below and tiny like a dark Ken doll along with our two camels from where I was sitting. I was only a small fraction, perhaps a quarter of the way up. As I sat there and gazed far out into the desert I saw other pyramids rising in the distance. I felt connected to the desert, with that pyramid and complete with my experience in Egypt. I could have traveled the thousands of miles from Michigan for that one moment, returned without a second more, and would have still felt content. Happy.

After the planes, the modern day noise and pollution of cities, the excitement of fireworks, a celebration with friends, the chaos of thieves and robbery, I felt risen above it all upon the pyramid. I had truly become a character from the "Choose Your Own Adventure" stories for it had been adventure in its purest form.

I felt unique in life to be sitting there, having an experience that very few would ever have. It was both an honor and humbling.

Spalding Gray encapsulated "a perfect moment" best by stating, "I always like to have one before I leave an exotic place. They're a good way of bringing things to an end. But you can never plan for one. You never know when they're coming. It's sort of like falling in love . . . with yourself."

It was a moment of peace and a moment of quiet. I certainly did not plan that afternoon nor did I ever dream the moment happening. Like the tree and the boy just being together in Silverstein's tale, I gazed into the distance of the expansive desert. It was my perfect moment. I fell in love with Egypt, the desert and myself, all one under the sun.

And although I was aware of time happening below, upon the pyramid, it ceased to exist. The Egyptians have a saying: "Men fear time, but time fears the pyramids." I intended to soak up every moment I could before my guide motioned from below to come down. So I slowly descended and climbed back onto my camel. After a tour of some ancient tombs and the Sphinx we returned to the guide's shop. Then I took a cab back to the center of Cairo.

I had not been in a mosque since arriving and was hoping to experience one before I left. Rising above the city there is a large mosque called the Muhammad Ali Pasha, or Alabaster Mosque. It is located in the Citadel of Cairo.

When the cab dropped me off I was the only white man while all the Egyptians went about their day around me. The neighborhood was sand brown in color. The stone homes were crowded next to each other with small alleys weaving in and out of different areas. The roads were not paved and the desert sand blew freely around.

There was a small square with a few benches around an old dried out fountain in the center. It served as a roundabout for the old trucks carrying many men piled in the bed for a ride. They shared the road with the horse and buggies that carried fruit and bread. I sat on one of the benches for a few minutes a bit terrified to continue exploring. I had no idea where I was as the dream continued.

I began walking up a dirt road that led up to the Citadel. As I approached the top I was informed that the mosque was closed for the day. People had begun setting up colorful decorations of paper lanterns and different colored plates and cups on long tables in the streets. It was time to feast after fasting all day as the sun began to set. It gave a very communal feel to the poor neighborhood that everyone came together in celebration.

I was disappointed I would not be able to see the inside of a mosque and went around to another side to try and get a better view. There was a similar dirt road that led up to a gate where five Egyptian men stood. One noticed me and approached.

He was tall and slender, about six feet with a black moustache. He was a casual and non-Hollywood glamorized version of Nick Arnstein, Omar Sharif's character in *Funny Girl*. He appeared to be in his mid to late thirties and wore an old, tattered and torn brown leather jacket over a black shirt with black denim pants. His eyes were calm and his energy non-evasive. But instantly I put up my guard because of my previous experience being robbed.

The robbery skewed my view of the culture and it was still tender. I felt jaded. But I tried to remember the thieves were just two people out of millions in Cairo and the incident wasn't a representation of the whole culture. I also recalled the nice Egyptians I had met and understood what little I had the majority of Egyptians had even less. But the thieves scarred me and were first in my thoughts with anyone new that entered the dream.

"What are you doing?" the man asked with curiosity.

"I was just trying to get a closer look at the mosque," I replied cautiously.

"Well this one is closed. But if you would like, I can take you to a spot that overlooks the city and the pyramids," he responded.

"That is alright," I replied. I figured he would expect some money for his services.

"Well if you walk down through the village you can find it," he said pointing. Then proceeded to give directions.

"Thank you." Then I repeated the directions back to him.

"Are you sure you would not like me to take you?" he asked. I paused, and something inside of me said, *Trust*.

Perhaps a spontaneous and adventuresome side developed in the magical backyard while reading the "Choose Your Own Adventure" stories, incubating through childhood and adolescence before emerging with my first trip to Europe. Never knowing where I would sleep or what would happen encouraged and intensified a more spontaneous and bold quality. It told me *to* talk to strangers and explore different worlds in many forms. Not only other lands but the worlds of others, as we all live in our own unique realities.

"OK," I replied. "But just to the lookout."

"Alright then," he said. "Follow me."

We walked down the hill and into the borough, wandering through many tight alleys that shielded the afternoon sun as we passed the village people. From the adult men and women we walked by I received cautious, lingering and expressionless looks.

But from the children sitting in the doorways, bare feet in the sand, their eyes grew wide with wonder at the visitor escorted through their streets. They made me feel like the Grand Marshal in a quiet parade-of-one. As the mini-ambassadors greeted me with their ritual chants of "hello" and "welcome."

It seemed like a labyrinth of passages through the homes. I felt as if I was being pulled deeper into the culture with a local's perspective. I did not feel unsafe. Every step was new. The explorer inside was more interested in allowing the experience to unfold.

The man guided me through the opening of a wall made of stones outside some homes. It rose seven feet, just above my head. Inside a hill was blanketed with knee-deep trash. Much of the trash was not contained in bags and included everything from food to appliances. I followed as he made his way through the rubbish to the top of the peak. Along the way many cats shopped for dinner, oblivious to us as we passed through.

I felt saddened for the people whose homes were so near. But I did not give a second thought about climbing the mound. The man didn't apologize for an instant for the neighborhood's appearance, as if accepting their lot in life. I also felt respected and accepted as a common local in being shown their way, not a nice, clean "tourist" path. It was very matter of fact, that this is the way we get there, and this is the way we're going.

After scaling to the top I turned to look. I was high above the village and could see the towers from many mosques rising throughout. The pyramids, including the one I had just climbed, appeared in the distance. I fell completely into the view. It was visually hypnotic like a snake charmer's music and mesmerized me for many moments. I nearly forgot I was not alone when I snapped out of my trance.

My guide was sitting behind me on a stone, still under the view's spell. The way he absorbed and admired the scene made me feel even more comfortable and at ease with him. He looked peaceful in his gaze like he too was experiencing it for the first time or was in the presence of a lover. He then came back to me.

"If you would like I know a mosque that I can take you to," he said.

"Alright," I said, the little voice inside instructing me to continue the trust. We began descending the hill toward the village.

"Look on the ground," he said. "Sometimes you can find little artifacts from many years ago. I found an old pipe the other day."

So we began sifting the ground with our feet, and squatted down if something caught our eye to examine it more closely. After a few moments he found a broken spout from a teapot.

"Here," he said. "A souvenir for you."

"Thank you," I said.

We arrived at a mosque and ascended the winding spiral staircase of one of the towers. It was very tight and confined inside. With each step darkness squeezed every ounce of light out like water from a wet rag. I never experienced such complete darkness and searched with my hands for the walls to brace myself as I rose. It seemed like we climbed hundreds of tiny steps before light appeared again at the top of the tower.

When we reached the top and walked out onto the small balcony the snake charmer's flute began its music as the reverie took over. The darkness from the tower and the robbery washed even further away into the past. My mind rose with my body to the top. Instead of spiraling downward from the mugging and creating a negative experience I escalated upwards, choosing to trust in a stranger again.

"You like what you see?" he asked.

"Yes, very much," I replied. "It is beautiful."

"Would you like to go have tea and continue?" he then asked like a question at the bottom page of a "Choose Your Own Adventure" book. I nodded, and we began descending the staircase.

He brought me to a small local café. It appeared more like a garage with a cement floor. It looked out upon the street with a handful of round, French café style tables and chairs for two scattered throughout. Seating also lined the outside entry to view the people and cars passing on the unpaved road. When we arrived, my guide approached a small, simple counter to the left. He knew the owner and they exchanged smiles and small talk as he ordered two cups of tea. We sat at a small table against the far wall. There was a small television mounted in the corner with a cartoon playing and the volume turned low.

"It is teaching about Ramadan," he said while pointing to the screen. "It is a time where you reflect on the year, find forgiveness with anyone throughout the year you had any conflict, so that you can start fresh with the New Year. Every morning from sun up to sun down you fast and pray. And at sundown everyone gathers together to feast." I nodded with understanding then noticed a man at another table smoking from a hookah pipe.

"Have you tried the hookah?" he asked. I shook my head no.

He returned to the counter and obtained a hookah from the owner then brought it to our table.

"It is a very light way to smoke," he said as he lit the coals. "You put the flavored tobacco on the fire and get a small taste of tobacco. It is not as heavy as smoking cigarettes."

The tobacco was a berry and apple flavor. I didn't realize I did it properly or inhaled anything until I exhaled and tasted the fruity hints. It was very light and felt like breathing out flavored air. It added another sense of scent to the experience.

"Do you like to smoke hash," he then asked. I smiled inside at the thought of the potential new direction the adventure was taking.

"Once or twice," I replied knowingly.

"Well I have a friend and if you like I could get some. We could go back to my home," he continued. "Would you like that?"

"Yes," I simply said. We finished our tea and left.

We walked through the alleys to a home with an outside foyer covered by part of the roof. The area was dark as night. I waited there as the man knocked on the door. His friend appeared and my guide went inside. They kept the door open and I could still see, although not hear them.

What are you doing?! I asked myself as I stood waiting while streaks of panic set in. *They could be in there planning to you knock you over the head and leave you for dead! And* nobody *in the world knows where you are.* But the calming voice inside said to continue to trust. Fear faded when my guide reappeared smiling.

"All set," he said. "Let us go."

When we arrived at his home I realized how modest his living was by its appearance. He mentioned he lived with his brothers and sisters and was eager to introduce me to them. But no one else was home.

It was very simple with stone walls and tiled floor to keep cool from the Egyptian sun. There was sand and dust from the street and a few carpets placed on the ground. A narrow hallway followed the entrance with a small kitchen to the left and a larger, open area ahead of us. His bedroom was to the right across from the kitchen.

As I entered his room he cleared off a chair next to the entrance for me to sit. He sat on his bed, covered in a sky blue blanket, and proceeded to roll the hash into four joints as we talked.

A small square window was cut into the stone on the wall in front of me that allowed in a muddled murmur of street noise, adding another sense to the experience. Even more so when he turned on an old radio that sat upon a nightstand in between us. A purely instrumental version of The Beatles' "Because" began playing. I was tickled that The Beatles found their way into the experience. He then began proudly showing me his collection of coins.

I was fascinated by his assortment of primarily Egyptian, but some Middle Eastern coins, especially since my collection of coins from the countries I visited beginning with my first overseas trip were mainly European. I could see they meant a great deal to him the way he enthusiastically spoke and shared different memories about them and where he received them. Most of which were gifts from his father. I was holding and admiring five coins with hieroglyphics, examining them closely. I was drawn to their detail and was lost in them for several minutes while he observed.

"Pick one," he eventually said. I was very excited but understood how important they were to him. They seemed the only thing of value, much of it sentimental, that he owned.

"No," I said. "It is your collection, I could not."

"You like?" he asked.

"Yes, very much," I responded. "They are amazing."

"Then pick one. Any one," he replied. I was so tempted and found one I really liked.

"How about this one?" I asked as I picked it up and showed it to him.

"Yes," he said. "It is yours."

"Thank you," I replied. "This means a lot to me."

"Here," he said as he reached for something from the table near his bed. "This is the pipe I found the other day. You may have it as well."

"Are you sure?" I asked.

"Yes," he replied. "I can find another one."

"In my culture," he continued, "whatever anybody has we share with those who do not. Everything is done in trade so that no one goes without. If my friend who is a cab driver does not have money to buy his tea, he trades a ride somewhere to the man that has given the tea. It is such a simple concept at the most basic level that is complicated by most. Share."

After he rolled all the hash up he lit a joint and passed it to me. As we became high the conversation turned to lighter subjects. He spoke of Omar Sharif and how proud he and his country were that one of their own succeeded in Hollywood. And of Umm Kulthum, an Egyptian singer, songwriter and actress from the 20's to the 70's whose songs lasted for hours. She was a national treasure, believed by many to be the greatest female singer in history of Arabic music. I had heard her around Cairo because she was still widely played throughout cafes and restaurants. Her voice produced a soothing and tranquil trance.

I began to feel very humbled by his kindness and the experience he was giving to me, taking the time to share himself and his culture. Day turned into night as we sat in his room. Muslim chants echoed in the neighborhood, traveling through the streets from old speakers mounted atop building corners outside. They added a meditative sound to the dream.

"Would you like to see another mosque?" he asked. "They will all be closed now but I know someone that will let us in." I nodded in agreement.

We walked to the gate of the Sultan Hussein mosque. Its size and presence was epic like I was approaching an omnipotent kingdom. The darkness and lack of humans around only added to its presence. He knew the man at the gate and they exchanged Arabic before allowing us into the courtyard. My guide pointed out a plaque just outside the door stating a brief history of the mosque with an English translation. He waited while I read it. I found it endearing he wanted to educate me on it as well.

As we entered we removed our shoes and placed them near the doorway. There was no one else inside. The intricately carved metal lantern lights hanging down from the ceiling were dimmed. But they were still raised several feet high above our heads.

It opened up into a large open space, the ground draped in Persian rugs of many different colors. Elaborately detailed tiles covered the walls. Nothing "matched" but it all worked together in its own unique way. The simplicity of the open space with no furniture of any kind along with pillars throughout rising to the ceiling balanced out the eclectic array of color in the walls and rugs. It took my breath away as the surreal experience with the man came to a crescendo. I felt so small in the vast space absorbing it all in as we quietly floated through.

The experience took on a dual effect. I felt in my own world experiencing the mosque. But at the same time I felt divine with a ubiquitous force, led by the man. I still at that point had not even asked his name. His identity to me at that moment was more like an angel guiding me along instead of an Egyptian man.

Each step I took I could feel the sacredness of the structure and the infinite amount of prayers that had been whispered within its walls for hundreds of years and sent to the sky. While the Muslim chants continued to echo throughout the city outside I experienced an out-of-body feeling. A transcendental presence of peace gently wrapped around me.

Feeling warm and aglow we entered a second room where the ceiling shimmered and shined with a gold color. I slowly turned in circles with my head to the sparkling sky. We never spoke. No words were needed. It was a moment simply to be a part of and to be felt.

After we left he suggested another cup of tea at the cafe. For our second visit we sat outside to watch life pass by.

"What is you name?" I finally asked.

"Muhammad," the prophet simply said, revealing his name. The same name as the mosque I attempted to explore hours before manifested in a person who brought me on an unexpected journey.

"Nice to meet you, I'm Jason," I said.

"Jason," he repeated slowly in his Arabic accent, making sure he pronounced it correctly. "Please tell me about you and your family."

"I come from a family of four boys," I began. "But one is deceased."

"What?" he asked with a confused look, attempting to understand.

"One passed away," I said in a different way.

Still he did not understand what I was trying to express while I thought of another way to communicate it.

"One is no longer living," I responded.

Then it clicked for him and in the most nonchalant way said, "Oh, he is with the gods. My father is with the gods."

He stated it so casually like Joe and his father had simply gone to the market. In that moment I felt a bit of peace inside with Joe's death and learning to live with it as the prophet Muhammed played his part.

"And what do you do in America?" he asked.

"I just completed school for the travel industry. I start working at a travel company that gives tours around the world when I return to America."

"Well have you enjoyed your tour of Egypt?" he asked.

"Yes, very much. I hoped to see a mosque but never imagined I would be given a gift like this," I said.

"Do you think other people would like to experience what you have?" he asked.

"To be shown around by a local is something I think many would enjoy," I said.

"Maybe we could start a business," he said with a playful smile. "You send them to me and I will show them what I have shown you."

"I'm sure it would be a success," I replied sincerely.

From there we lost ourselves in small talk. The kind of talk you don't even remember how you arrived at each topic because once it flowed into the next, the previous was forgotten. But it always connected.

I was in such shock by the entire afternoon and evening that I surrendered and allowed him to lead the experience. I felt my heart beat slow but strong. I wanted the amazing adventure to continue. But in the back of my mind I knew, just like when asleep and dreaming, that it was time to "wake up". I had to pack and fly from one world and time into another. It was overwhelming. And I still had no idea where I was or how far away my hotel was.

I did learn a few things about him but soon forgot, not out of disrespect, simply from pure shock. I was dually feeling calm and peaceful on the outside but frantic with excitement over what was happening on the inside. I tried to scribble down his name and address. Although he could speak English fairly well, when I handed him my journal to write his information down he informed me he could not write English. He tried to pronounce it as clearly as he could so I could phonetically write it down. But my hand was shaking so much that I could not write English either or later read my own handwriting. All I know of him:

Muhammad Almas
3
Somewhere near the Citadel
Cairo, Egypt.

After what felt like hours I told him I was flying out early the next morning and needed to go pack. A friend of his who owned a cab was at a table near us and Muhammad had him bring me back to my hotel. He accompanied me as we both entered the back seat.

"Do you need a ride to the airport," Muhammad asked.

"Yes, but it is very early that I need to be there."

"What time would you like to leave your hotel?" he asked.

"One in the morning," I said.

"I will be here," he replied.

I ran up to my hotel room amazed and humbled by the experience over the previous hours. In the time I spent with Muhammad my view of his country did a 180-degree turn. I was astounded with the culture and the people.

At one I brought my bags down and looked out the hotel's front door. As promised, Muhammad was present, waving and smiling. On the ride to the airport I stared out the window lost in thought and overflowing with humbled gratitude for the amazing four days. It was a quick visit but I felt I received so much.

"Did you enjoy your time in Egypt?" Muhammad asked.

I heard him but was in such reflection I was barely able to speak. There was a pause in my answer before I turned to him, only able to stutter, "Yes, yes."

"You did not have to answer," he said. "Your eyes already answered for you."

On the ride, he presented me with some gifts he had brought. One was a painted papyrus leaf with an Egyptian goddess and the others were Egyptian stamps and more coins.

"It signifies protection of the home," he said of the papyrus. "Hang it wherever you may call home and it will be protected. And here, I bring one more thing."

He reached into his jacket and pulled out the last joint.

"It will make your flight nicer," he said as he lit it. I laughed. We smoked. Then we sat in silence for the rest of the trip simply enjoying each other's company.

When we reached the airport he helped me with my bags out of the cab. I reached in my pocket and grabbed about $7 in Egyptian Pounds. I extended my hand with the money in it.

"Thank you so much for *everything,"* I said as he reached out to shake my hand. When he realized there was money in it he acted very surprised and pulled away.

"It is not necessary," he said, "I did not do this for anything in return."

"I know," I responded. "But please accept as a small gesture of thanks."

We parted ways and I entered the airport. I boarded the plane eager to get some beauty sleep before my third date with Amsterdam.

7

"Dallas!" I exclaimed, shocked to discover my friend inside The Globe. "How did you manage to find me?"

Dallas had returned to Guildford for the Millennium. We planned to meet in Amsterdam but failed to sort out the details beforehand. I hoped to borrow money from him before returning to America because I was still having problems with my credit card.

I'd spent the morning shuffling between the currency exchange at the train station and a phone booth talking with the credit card company. Because I had not used the emergency credit card for over two years since my first trip to Europe my account was automatically frozen for protection when atypical advances were requested in Cairo. After satisfying extensive identity questions and waiting for an authorization fax from my bank in America to reach the bank in Europe I finally received a much-needed cash advance.

"I thought you may have checked into the same hostel we stayed at last time," Dallas said.

"I *just* put my name in an hour ago," I said, "but if I didn't come back with some money they couldn't hold it."

"Well good timing then, just like Guildford, remember?" he replied. "Come on, my friend is waiting at a nearby coffeeshop.

"You wouldn't believe the hoops I had to jump because of what happened in Cairo," I said, excited to tell him the whole story.

"Come on, we have to get going," he repeated as if he didn't even hear me.

My whirlwind experience with Muhammad occurred not even ten hours earlier. I was dying to share the experience with someone. I needed to hear it aloud to make it feel real.

"Dallas! Wait a second! You'll never believe what happened to me in Cairo!" I said louder. He continued ahead of me with his hands in his pockets, bundled up from the winter air.

"Jason it's cold," Dallas said. "We're almost there. Tell me inside."

We arrived at the Three Stooges coffeeshop, a prophecy of sorts. Dallas's friend was waiting inside.

"Jason this is Ewan," Dallas introduced us. "We met at school when I studied in Guildford."

"Hi. Nice to meet you," I said rather quickly and shook his hand. I wasn't trying to be rude but my attention was focused on wanting to relive and share the Egyptian dream.

The three of us ordered drinks at the bar and then brought them to a table.

"Ok, *now* will you listen to what happened to me in Cairo?" I began. I was about to burst.

Dallas lit a joint and handed it to me. "Yes. But first take a hit and calm down.

So I did. "Jason just got back from Egypt."

"Really!" Ewan said and turned to me. "How was it?"

I went to pass the joint to Ewan and froze on his face. It was like I just realized he existed and I immediately crushed on him. Staring back at me was a very attractive man in his early twenties. Ewan's background was French and Scottish. He had brown eyes and short brown hair gelled like a 1940's solider, parted at the side. His body was fit and his face was angular with a five o'clock shadow.

I loved the intense attention such a handsome man was giving me. The whole Egyptian trip story erupted out of me like a geyser to the new person joining the adventure. I only took a breath when Dallas or Ewan passed me the joint.

But even as the pot's effect sunk in I couldn't slow down. I began talking dramatically faster. My hands flung through the air. I felt so blown away from the recent life-changing experience. It had to come out.

There was something very open about Ewan's gaze. It contained a genuine curiosity and interest. It instantly made me feel comfortable. The entire time I talked he was focused on my every word. He listened, really listened to me. He maintained constant eye contact. I was drawn to him. I felt understood and connected.

I had met a fellow traveler. He too was an active participant in life, whether his own experiences or via someone else's. Through his father's job he lived in South Africa and Columbia during his childhood. His exposure to different ways of life from vastly different countries and continents began early. It shined through in his openness. Even though he lived in England, I instinctively felt he would play a part in my life. And it surprised me how confident I felt about it.

Over the following few days, Dallas and I indoctrinated Ewan to all things Amsterdam. We showed him our favorite coffeshops and presented him the best treats to sample. We exposed him to all the video booths and the red light district. Together we window-shopped the ladies lit in red. Then broke off to make our purchase. Dallas was all about it with no hang-ups because it *was* legal. I couldn't tell if Ewan was really into it. But we all had private time to decide what we wanted and I always snuck into the booths for the gay porn. When we convened to discuss our acquisitions I couldn't lie that I made one—only give reasons why I didn't. But never the real one—she didn't have a penis.

When our short time in Amsterdam ended I was sad to see Ewan go. A good friendship began. Unfortunately he lived thousands of miles away from Michigan. I knew I would see him again. One day. But I assumed it would be years.

The trip to both Egypt and Amsterdam opened my eyes. It gave small whispers that spoke of the good in life and people again. It confirmed how alive I felt while traveling.

After I returned to Michigan I began my internship at the travel company. It was a typical nine-to-five office-cubicle job. The same kind I rejected in Chicago. But it was temporary. At least I tried and experienced it. Regardless, I was excited to explore the industry, gain some experience for my resume, and see if it was a fit.

Luckily I was the assistant to a pretty blonde a year older than me. We formed a brother/sister-like relationship through sharing a cubicle. I affectionately called her Little One. It helped tremendously to have another body in the "cell".

My job was to make sure the tour members' details were correct for their flights and print their tickets. Most of the tours were to Europe as the owner was Dutch. As I printed out numerous tickets back to Europe, many to Amsterdam, I drooled with desire to return. I deeply wanted to spend more time there.

I missed the consciousness of people I met abroad. Their perspective of life resonated with me. I felt there was far more openness and acceptance toward differences in life and people. Perhaps with such a small concentration of many different cultures in an area smaller than America, Europeans were naturally exposed to and brought up with different lifestyles. And as foreigners easily traveled in and out of other countries because of proximity it provided more familiarity to other ways of living, whether they agreed or not with certain beliefs and viewpoints.

Realistically I knew not everyone would be completely copacetic with diversity of lifestyles and it depended upon being raised respectfully. But an underlying foundation of awareness seemed to be present.

With such a vast land that America is, cultures and differences are easily lost. There seemed only one way to live life offered, at least within my upbringing in the Midwest. The sheltered, conservative Catholic rearing didn't portray another. Even Hollywood and fairytales taught the same. Boy marries girl. When I tasted a more general acceptance in Europe, I wanted a bigger bite.

The life I was presented with was simply not enough anymore. All I knew was I was just beginning to feel like I could breathe again on my travels. I craved another refuge.

After two months I was allowed to take a holiday before the busy travel season started. I wanted to go back to Europe for a breath of air. It didn't matter to me where. But finances were limited after Egypt and Amsterdam. It seemed unattainable.

Fortunately working at a travel company had some perks. Flight deals often flew into the office. One afternoon Little One discovered an inexpensive ticket to London. I immediately e-mailed Ewan:

I know we've only known each other briefly. But I have a chance to come to England. Would it be all right if I stayed with you to save money?

I felt confident asking; trusting a bond was made in Amsterdam. He confirmed it by welcoming me into his home that he shared with his girlfriend Gemma. So I left in March 2000 for ten days. Secretly, somehow, I hoped a miracle door would open to keep me there.

I arrived in England late in the night and Ewan met me at the train station in Guildford. I had not been there since I stayed with Dallas. Ewan had prepared an extra room in their home for me and after a brief reunion we went to sleep.

In the morning I was awoken to a knock on my door. A beautiful, buxom, blond bombshell with porcelain skin burst into my room. Her long extensions were pulled high atop her head in a ponytail with her bangs curled and make-up painted like a pin-up girl to rival Bettie Page or any other on the side of a WWII plane.

"Good morning! Good morning! I'm Gemma. Ewan has told me all about you! Nice to meet you! Would you like a cup of tea?" she said in one breath.

"I'm Jason, tea would be nice, thank you," I said while laughing at the bright bubbly creature that awoke me into the next dream.

Ewan and Gemma's hospitality blew me away. They were attentive and made sure I felt at home, coordinating their schedules so that one or the other was available to show me around and spend time with me. They introduced me to their friends. Ewan often made his signature student meal—toasted bread topped with tomato and cheese, melted to perfection in the oven. And my teacup never went dry. It seemed it was always teatime. They were two beautiful people full of life and fun.

One evening Ewan, who was also a DJ, performed at the Student Union. Gemma and I spent the night dancing to Ewan's spinning. Afterward he continued to spin at an after party in one of their schoolmate's flat, while Gemma retired home.

In the early morning hours Ewan and I were walking home to the sounds of birds chirping as the sun began to rise. I wanted to share a bit about why I felt so drawn to Europe. Still fearing rejection, I didn't want to mention Joe. But there wasn't any way around Joe since he was the catalyst for it all.

So I mentioned very quickly that I had a brother who died. And Ewan just listened. Like at the coffeeshop in Amsterdam, but with a tender ear. It felt amazing to speak of Joe and have someone *just listen.* A good friendship rooted deeper.

On my last night in England, Ewan, Gemma and I went into London for a night of dancing to send me off in style and celebrate our meeting and time together. Dallas always shared with me the amazing nights he had at the clubs in London. I was hoping to experience one of my own. Gemma found a flyer for a new club called Fabric and heard that it was quite good. So we went.

We had each taken an ecstasy pill and the drug kicked in. The club was crowded and the music loud. I was feeling a euphoric bliss, a love for life and everyone around, especially the beautiful angels known as Ewan and Gemma.

The pill gave the night a feeling of love. Simply love. The combined body heat and sweat of the packed club created holes in my heart's dry ice vault. Its mass continued to change from solid to hazy fog. The drug may have manufactured the feeling but I needed to feel the beauty in life again and the drug assisted.

At what felt like the peak of the evening and feeling from the pill Gemma came up to me and asked me to dance. She wrapped her arms around my neck and we both smiled as we moved our sweat-drenched bodies together. It felt fun, liberating, and was a moment of connection with her through dance. Then she looked me in the eyes.

"Ewan told me you had a brother that died," she said. Her words took me completely by surprise. I didn't know what to say.

"Yes," I replied.

"How?" she asked.

"In a car accident," I said.

"I'm sorry to hear. But I bet you he's up in heaven right now jealous that you're having the time of your life in a London club," she responded in a cute and endearing tone.

"Probably." Then I paused and thought about it for a second. "Actually he's probably here dancing with us. He was a dancer," I said still feeling in love with life. She got a surprised look on her face.

"Oh you're probably right!" she exclaimed. Then in the most eternally touching expression turned her head to the right to "look" for him. In that moment it felt like a force turned my head the other way and a brush of energy came rushing past me filled with warmth. It shook me to the core like a shockwave. It was a split second. Then I turned back to Gemma's eyes.

"I say we have a dance for Joe," she said with a smile.

"That sounds perfect," I said smiling back as the genuine love for Gemma grew.

"This one is for you Joe!" she shouted to the sky. I kept smiling. Then Ewan approached.

"Hey, what are you doing dancing so close with my girlfriend?" he playfully said.

"We're dancing a dance for Joe," she turned to Ewan and proudly said. I just kept grinning at how adorable of a creature she was to me.

"Great, can I join in?" Ewan asked.

"Of course," we both replied as the three of us huddled in a dance for Joe. I felt a safe, warm feeling hovering above us.

8

After returning to America my desire to spend more time in Europe exponentially exploded. The trips weren't enough. Now I wanted to live there. I wanted to surround myself with people like Ewan and Gemma. I felt living abroad allowed me *to live*. It provided distance, which created the freedom to choose the life I wanted. Not the one I was instructed. The friends I met overseas gave the type of support that felt right.

So I found a semester program at a university in London, which had an internship opportunity in the travel industry. It felt meant to be. I hoped to gain more experience and network. But I also secretly yearned to get back for the clubs and drugs. My heart desperately ached for another meeting with Joe.

The university assigned me to a small British travel company for the upcoming fall semester of 2000. I committed even though the expense was beyond by means. But I continued to work at the Michigan travel company by day and Noto's by night. My hunger and obsession to find a way to live in Europe consumed me. A new dream was established.

To focus on my goal, I closed myself off from other people. I built up walls fearing rejection if they knew who I was becoming. For months from spring into summer I became a robot working as much as I could. When the role of brother or son was needed I turned the autopilot on, said the lines, and played the part.

But soon the backdrop of Michigan and America became mentally exhausting and suffocating. The pressure and inherent expectations of my old life squeezed me. I perpetually felt like I was underwater and unable to hold my breath another second as I counted down the days to escape.

Sometimes I desperately needed to come up for air and sample the life my heart craved. So I would drive an hour to a club near Michigan State for a one-night stand about once a month. It always involved alcohol to release my inhibitions about physically interacting with men. But drinking grew old and felt too harsh on my body. And when the rendezvous was through my guilt and confusion pulled me back underwater. Deeper. Darker.

It felt vital to find another escape before *the* escape to Europe, which seemed so far away. I wanted to go home. But I didn't understand where it was or what it meant anymore. The magical backyard was gone. The person I shared it with was dead. And what my religion taught home should be with a man and woman persecuted my feelings and desires for men. Plagued with confusion, I yearned to remain numb.

An answer came one evening when I returned early from Noto's. Nobody was home. The toll of working two jobs caught up with me. I was tired. Tired of being a prisoner in the vault and of dealing with it all. I wanted to break out from its chambers.

Frustration raged like fire. It created a whiteout, knocking me to my knees. My heart's tears dropped to the dry ice vault, changing more of the solid to cloudy gas. It was all mentally and emotionally asphyxiating. I searched my parent's bathroom for painkillers. Then washed one down with a drink. That was the night when the idea of slowly letting go—first in spirit—of life became slightly more attractive. Easier.

The painkillers were the quick and easy fix to get me through the remaining months before England. Between two physically aging parents with aches and pains there seemed a plethora of pills available. Work and sleep. That was all I wanted to focus on and pills did the job. Problem solved. It felt like a logical solution. It wasn't all the time, never a routine, just when I *needed* it. So I never thought it was a big deal.

I was very careful. I kept track of which pills from which bottles I took. I wanted to make sure one source wasn't completely depleted or make it obvious that some were missing. My parents never found out or questioned my activities. The portrayal of the old Jason remained consistent with what they knew.

As my departure date approached there were two Jasons going to England. One was the image of a happy-go-lucky Jason. The image that everybody knew, saw, and who was attempting to build a career in the travel industry. The other Jason was a sad and lonely soul looking for a way out of the world or a connection to the next. In the dual lives I was living I didn't even know how it would turn out. Although I secretly hoped for the latter when I departed for England at the beginning of October 2000.

After landing in London I traveled to Guildford to reunite with Ewan and Gemma. They were still living together and in their third year of university. It was precious to me knowing such warm and giving people were near. I felt welcome and like I always had a home with them, if needed. A few days later I boarded the train for the city to begin my adventure.

I arrived at Baker Street, famous as the neighborhood of Sherlock Holmes. It would be my Underground stop to my London home each day. I picked up my keys from the university just before it closed on a Friday afternoon. They informed me I would be sharing the flat with four other people and said it was an eleven-minute walk from the university. I learned whenever I asked for directions from Londoners they gave it with precise minutes.

When I opened the door at 105 Crawford Street, Flat #3 it was empty. The place was on the third story (fourth floor in America) and contained three bedrooms. It lined a street full of buildings rising mostly to the same level. The neighborhood had cafes, salons, convenience stores, and a cinema scattered around and mixed in with homes. An Arabic market across the street from my home provided quick food runs.

All of my flatmates had arrived before me and picked a room. I was left with a twin bed pushed tight against a wall. My mystery roommate already claimed the more comfortable double bed in the room. But that didn't matter to me. All that did was I accomplished my dream and was going to be *living* in Europe!

My first night I spent alone walking the streets. I wanted to immediately breathe in as much of the city as I could. It was a way to bond with London, my home for the next two and a half months. I was able to save some money but I would need to be on a tight budget. As I walked the streets I pictured myself doing a great job at the internship. I trusted from there a door would open to create a new life in Europe. But

I was also salivating to return to the clubs and drugs desperate for another appearance by Joe.

I was the first to arrive back to the flat that night and went to sleep. I was awoken when the others came in during the late hours and crawled into their beds. The next morning everyone woke before me and started their day. Eventually I walked out of my bedroom to meet the people I would share the adventure and home.

One by one as they opened their mouths I was surprised and confused when I heard nothing but American accents. Tim and Josh (my roommate) were from Wisconsin, Miles from New York, and Nathan from Los Angeles. I signed up to room with international students from other countries. I wanted an escape from *all* things American. So I immediately put up a wall between The Americans and myself.

It didn't block the genuine impulse to treat them kindly. But rather prevented them from being able to get to know much about me. I was not open to sharing my life anymore with America. Once classes for them began and city work life started for me it became easier because I did not see much of them and tried to make sure they didn't see much of me.

For work I took the Bakerloo line to Oxford Circus then switched to the Central line and got off at Tottenham Court Road. It was rarely more than thirty minutes before I arrived at a building near the British Museum. Inside contained the one room headquarters of The Magical Tour Company.

My boss Patrick was a short Irish man with a round belly, glasses, and a dark full beard with bits of gray. He was an honest businessman trying to provide for his family. He employed a middle-aged English man named Andrew as his office manager and an American girl on a work visa as an assistant. If Patrick wasn't in the office he could be found at his other location, the pub around the corner. He would go there to work in peace or conduct meetings, always with his favorite drink, a pint of Guiness.

"It's pretty straightforward," Patrick explained on my first day in a thick Irish accent. It was difficult to understand him at first but I gradually learned to decipher what he was saying. "We give day and weekend tours around the UK and mainland Europe."

"Alright," I said as he began showing me different flyers for the tours.

"Stonehedge, Oxford, Paris, Amsterdam. There's a tour to Dublin, Edinburgh, stuff like that. Basically the main tourist spots and capitals of Europe."

"So what does my job entail?" I asked.

"Well we market primarily to international students studying abroad at the different universities and schools around central and greater London," he replied as he sat down and began writing on the back of one of the flyers.

"Andrew handles signing people up and collecting payment. Becky assists in whatever else needs to be done. You will mainly be delivering flyers to the schools and talking to their activities directors to help promote the tours." He stood and handed me the flyer he wrote on.

"Start with these schools for today. Take the Underground or bus. Do you have a tube pass?"

"I was going to get a monthly one."

"Well here, take this," he said, reaching into his wallet and handing me ten pounds. "Get yourself a day pass for today and pick up an *A to Z*. Use mine for today, it has every London street in it.

My eyes grew wide. I felt like a baby bird thrust out of its nest into the jungle of *London* on my first day. It was a little intimidating to be expected to just find my way around to the long list of schools. I thought I would be lucky to get to a few of them.

"Do you have a mobile?" he asked.

"No," I replied. He opened a drawer and pulled one out

"Here," he said. "This is a spare. You can use it while you're in London. Call if you have any questions or get lost."

I began to laugh inside. The probability of getting lost was strong. It certainly wasn't the cubicle internship I expected. But at least I was able to be outside.

"And take one of the umbrellas in the corner if you didn't bring one. It will probably rain at some point," he added. I grabbed one and made my way to the door. "And have fun!"

So it began. Every day Patrick gave me a list of places to deliver flyers. I spent hours on the Underground, bus, or walking to promote the tours.

After work I returned to the flat, quickly made dinner, then went back out into the streets even though I was exhausted from all the walking throughout the day. I tried to avoid being home while The Americans were there.

It usually worked out. Their classes were late in the morning and they had a desire for pub fun at night. So they often slept in, while I snuck out early in the morning as part of the rush hour crowd on the Underground going to work. And the evenings were left for exploring.

I purposely became lost in the maze of streets and remained gone for hours. But I would not give up until I found my way back to the flat. I would typically slip into bed before my flatmates returned from the pubs, sensitive to the warning sounds of the old lift opening and key in the lock. If I were already asleep I would always be awakened to the after party of people in our living room on the other side of my wall. To me they were the loud Americans that I continued to put up walls between. And my spirit slowly and quietly continued to let go.

But there was one thing the Americans and I shared—an interest in the music and club life of London. And the drugs that accompanied it. A week into the semester Miles made an inexpensive ecstasy connection through a classmate. It was a real bargain at four pounds per pill.

I simply put my order in to Miles each week from the comfort of our flat. Then waited while he delivered it back home. It could not have been made easier or more effortless. The Americans and I would occasionally go clubbing together. But I was more interested in the music and dancing, while hoping Joe would make an appearance.

In truth I enjoyed The Americans company. They were good people. But they remained external relationships and only for the nights clubbing. Knowing what was beneath their surface didn't hold much interest to me.

The evening walks were also a way I unconsciously tried to tire myself out to escape the dry ice vault and the emptiness and loneliness I felt inside. New stimulations and getting lost occupied my mind and my time. But it was only a temporary external fix as wherever I went the loneliness followed like a loyal companion. I had reached a point of mental, emotional, and spiritual fatigue from trying to understand why Joe died and *I* was the one still living. The exhaustion also came from trying to cling onto the life I was *told* to live. But I was dying inside. I didn't feel any purpose for me to be on earth. There was no love for myself and therefore no love for my life.

One evening I took a shortcut through Hyde Park. I began to notice many men wandering around the southeast corner near the Rose Garden. Intuitively I knew I had discovered an area where men cruised for sex.

I noticed a man pause and stop as he looked at me. Then he went off the path into a bush through an opening. Nervous excitement bubbled and surged like lava. An erotic pulse beat like a tribal drum. The silhouetted beings' desire was like sonar, beeping, honing in on a match to meet their need for the night, whether a kiss, a fuck, or something more.

Instead of feeling fear I was captivated to stay. It felt primal, like I was among my own kind. The fear of anyone stealing my money or causing me harm faded. There was something more important floating in the air—a hunger for human touch. Man to man.

Whether sexually erotic, passionate, sensual or animalistic it was the only thing on the agenda of the men led by libido. It felt liberating. I didn't know what would happen or even if I was in the market for anything. All I knew was that I'd found the ultimate freedom to explore. Do anything. *Be* anything. Be . . . me.

I entered the bush. A tall, handsome man with a swimmer's build in his thirties instantly began touching and kissing me ravenously. Like we were lovers reunited after years apart. He paused to take a deep, lingering look in my eyes. It was a moment of connection. Assurance to each other that intimacy was the intent, not harm.

He then quickly slid both his hands up underneath my shirt while I unbuttoned my pants and pulled my aroused cock out. He lowered his head to nibble my nipple before dropping to his knees. He unzipped his own pants and stroked himself while he took me in his mouth. I placed my hands on the back of his head and guided him in and out. His speed accelerated like a runner in the final stretch as he took me in and out faster, sucking more intently. It wasn't long before we both came like two prisoners released from solitary confinement. I zipped up my pants, thanked him, and left. In the moments of being with him I muzzled my mind. And simply felt. Freshness flourished inside for the life I did not think I was allowed.

As I walked through the park on my way out I was aware the man was not far behind. He was at my left heading in the same direction. I ached for more of an experience in that other life. But was far too insecure to imagine how to achieve it.

It seemed like the man was following me. I slowed my pace and noticed him accelerate his, closing the gap between us. As I approached a large tree I sensed he was attempting to interact with me again. My hunger growled for more, temporarily winning. I stopped at the tree. With my confirmation for round two, he rushed in like a breaking wave. He pressed his body against mine, pinning me against the tree, then passionately kissed me again.

"What is your name?" he whispered with a French accent into my ear.

"Michael," I lied. Not wanting to be Jason.

"What are you doing in London?" he asked attempting to make eye contact.

"I'm a student," I replied, careful not to reveal too much information.

"I am Baptiste," he said. "You are very beautiful." I looked down and didn't respond. Disbelief engulfed me. I did not feel beautiful any way, outside or in.

"I would like to see you again," he continued. "Will you meet me here next Sunday, at this spot?" I tried to think of a reason or excuse to decline. But the urge for more was stronger.

"I don't know," I said. I kept my responses short. I still felt very shy speaking to a man I was just physically intimate with.

"Well I will be here at 9:00 p.m." he said. "If you come that would make me very happy. But if not that is alright as well." There was no pressure in his gentle, respectable tone.

"Maybe," I said. "I need to get going."

"Hope to see you Beautiful Baby," Baptiste replied with my cheeks in his hands. We kissed one last time.

"Bye," I said.

"*Au revoir*," he responded.

As soon as I left the darkness of the park and was in the light of the city I tried to molt the experience like a snake shedding its skin. I vowed not to return to the park.

But as the week began my desire not to be home persisted. I continued to walk the streets each night for hours. And my desire for more interaction with men grew stronger. It quickly turned a visit to the park into the nightcap of my walking ritual.

The two lives I was living remained independent of one another. I could not perceive them as one. I still firmly believed I would have and conduct a life that was not gay.

Part of me felt shame for having sex with men. Like an abusive lover, it punched with all of its strength and knocked the wind out of me each time I experimented with a man, essentially mentally bullying myself. I was brainwashed to believe I was doing something morally wrong. I was lonely. I didn't like who I was, yet felt trapped.

My new life felt it had to hide out in the darkness of a park, like an animal. I loathed feeling like an animal. It was as if I was not equal to other people and could not live a life with dignity.

But simultaneously an awakening part of me loved feeling like an animal. It was the only thing that felt primal and in order with *my* human nature. It allowed me to explore intimate and physical contact with men wherever the opportunity presented itself. Each time I did it broke another of the dictator's controlling chains.

A battle was being fought inside me—one side pushing with all of its strength to open the door toward renewed life, while the other was pushing just as hard on the other side to keep it closed. There simply was not enough room for two lives in one body. Fearful original me believed it would be the end of its life. Unable to understand they were one in the same.

Each night I left the park, I swore it would be the last. But a longing for more of a connection with a man beyond the physical level was evolving.

When Sunday evening arrived I still had not decided whether or not to meet Baptiste. My mind paced between fear and desire as I sat home alone. I waited to the last possible moment to make a decision taking into account the traveling time needed to arrive at the meeting point by nine o'clock. The concern that one of my flatmates could arrive any minute and question where I was going if I *did* leave caused me to dash out the door. Once I hit the street and night air the curiosity to discover what was on the next page of my story with the Frenchman rushed me to the park.

I returned to the tree where I last saw Baptiste. He was not there when I arrived. I instantly felt rejection. But I stayed for a few minutes.

There was a man in the distance walking toward me with a bike. I was not sure if it was the Frenchman but waited. Dictator shouted to leave, instilling fear. But my desire to stay persisted. The approaching man made a slight turn, directly for the tree. It was Baptiste.

"I was not sure if it was you," he said as he stopped by the tree. "I did not think you would come. It is nice to see you." He smiled sweetly and went in for a kiss.

"Thank you," I replied.

"I am so happy that you came," he repeated then wrapped his arms around me and gave a warm and gentle squeeze. "I live about a ten minute walk from here. Would you like to come back to my flat?"

"Sure," I said, still shy to say much more. Unbeknownst to me we walked along a section of the park known as Lovers Lane.

"So how was your week?" he casually asked.

"It was alright," I responded.

"Just alright?" he said. "You seem a bit sad. Is everything okay?"

"I went clubbing the other night and spent too much of this week's budget," I said. "I'm just a little worried."

"Well did you have fun?" he asked.

"Yes, some. But I am upset that I was not very responsible."

"Well as long as you had fun do not worry," he said. "Things always find a way of working out."

It felt intimate to share something so personal to a stranger. But I already had enough anxiety over other issues and needed to open up to someone. There was something about his energy that made me comfortable.

He lived near Bayswater Underground station, not far from the park. I was nervous when we entered his home. Like my trip home with Uno I did not know what to expect.

In Baptiste's bedroom, the dim glow of a single lamp on a nightstand gave the only light. We began to gently kiss and slowly undress one another while standing at the side of the bed. His hair was black and parted at the side. His bangs swayed with his movements and felt soft as it brushed against my skin. His body was well-built with minimal body hair on his chest and around his nipples. At around 6'1" he was slightly taller than me.

He was extremely sensual as he assuredly ran his hands across my body. Then he knelt before me and took my cock in his mouth while his left hand went around to caress my ass. His right hand pulled open the top drawer of the nightstand then reached in and pulled out a condom.

Baptiste rose to his feet and continued to kiss me while he put the condom on me. Once on he turned his back to me. As I entered him and began to thrust I clutched and squeezed his built pectorals. I hugged my body toward his then turned my left cheek to rest on his back. I paused for a moment and just held him. Simply felt him and felt being *inside* him. I sensed his head turn to the right. I lifted mine off his back and placed my hand gently on his cheek to pull his lips closer to mine. With his country's kiss complete we both bent slightly forward and gave into the passion. As I moved my hips faster he began stroking his cock and placed his other hand on the bed to prop himself up. Soon he came. When he did he brought his hand back up to catch it and then waited until I came.

Then we climbed into bed and lied above the sheets while he spooned me. My racing mind returned to worrying about money and shame over what I had just done. I did not want to look him in the eyes and see myself naked in bed with another nude man. But at the same time I yearned to stay and feel it.

"Are you alright?" Baptiste finally said after a long silence.

"Yes," I said. It was a lie.

"Do you need anything?" he asked. I thought for a moment.

"Could you just run your fingers over my body please?" I responded.

"Of course, Beautiful Baby," he said with his disarming French accent. It was a term of endearment that poetically flowed from his lips.

He brushed his fingers all over my body. It helped relax me. I wanted to silence my thoughts and just feel.

"Stay with me tonight," Baptiste whispered while he continued to touch me. I began to think of an excuse.

"I can't," I said. "I have class early in the morning and must finish some homework."

"Ah you are so beautiful," he said. "I could easily fall in love with you."

I couldn't fathom how or why. Love for myself did not exist.

"Please just stay the night with me," he asked again, his accent gliding with a pining tone. I was tempted. I felt so comfortable in Baptiste's bed. But fear The Americans would question why I did not come home tortured me.

"I have to get up very early and need a good night sleep," I said.

"I will wake you and make sure you are not late," he said.

"I'm sorry, I can't," I replied. Then began to get up and dress. "Thank you though, you've been very kind."

"Can I see you again?" Baptiste asked leaning up from bed.

"I don't know," I said.

"Well let me give you my number, if you choose to spend more time together," he continued as he jumped out of bed to grab a paper and pencil. He wrote his details down and handed it to me.

"Thank you," I said.

"Do you know how to get home from here?" he asked.

"Yes. Au revoir, merci," I said as I walked toward the door.

"Wait," he said. Then went back into the bedroom. "Here take this." He offered me some money.

"No, I can't," I said.

"Please," he insisted. "I want you to eat this week."

"I will be fine," I said.

"But you will still worry and I do not want that, so please, take it," he said.

"Thank you," I said as I accepted it and clutched it in my hand. I opened the door and kissed him goodbye.

"Sweet dreams to you, Beautiful Baby," he said.

When I arrived at the Underground platform I looked in my palm. There was a twenty-pound note. The thought my body was *worth* something excited me. It made me feel happy that I contained some significance. But then shame for considering selling my body snuck in and the thought was left on the platform when I stepped on the train.

A week later I ventured on my own from The Americans to a gay club called Heaven. After dancing in the sexually charged atmosphere all-night and coming down from a pill, I wished to share intimacy with someone. Outside of the dark park.

As I left the club the rain poured on a cold autumn night. The memory of Baptiste's warm bed and his warmer energy resurfaced. I found cover in a red phone booth to call him.

"Hello?" Baptiste said.

"It's Michael," I replied.

"Ah, Beautiful Baby, how are you? *Where* are you?"

"I was clubbing at Heaven," I said. "I'm outside in a phone booth. Would you like some company?"

"Oh I would love to see you. But my sister is visiting from Paris," he responded. "Can I see you another time?"

"I don't know," I said. "I have to get going."

"Where are you going?" he asked. I quickly hung up the phone.

My low self-esteem interpreted his response as rejection. My own lies I was living in produced distrust. I questioned if he was telling me the truth. My insecure thoughts told me his "sister" was really another man already in his bed.

As the rain turned to a sprinkle, loneliness led me to the park. I never called Baptiste again. While my growth in connecting to a man beyond the physical stalled, in the park I remained.

As October ended the downward spiral continued. Nights at the clubs and taking ecstasy increased, as did the number of pills I would swallow. My body quickly built up a tolerance. I needed more pills to produce the effect that one used to give.

The ecstasy also suppressed my appetite. I evolved into a diet of tea, toast, cigarettes, and pills. Occasionally I would treat myself to different European chocolate bars such as Time Out and Flake at the vending machines while waiting on the platform for my train during work to the next school.

When I did have a proper meal once or twice a week it was usually traditional English bangers and mash that I topped with peas and beef gravy made from Oxo brand stock cubes. But I was happy the lifestyle allowed me to save money on food.

More for drugs I thought with no concern to my physical health. It trailed behind mental and emotional.

The drugs had a silver lining. It created the feeling life was still worth living. As I met and danced with interesting people from all over the world during spellbinding nights in the clubs, my soul was stirred. Thoughts of the next night clubbing kept me going Monday through Friday to get me to the weekend. Which meant I chose life for another week. It was progress. I was taking baby steps in choosing life again.

Occasionally I visited my adoptive family in Guildford whenever I needed a break from the city. I'd leave during the week just for a night so the weekends could be saved for the clubs. I would always be exhausted when I arrived from everything that was going on in the city. But my fatigued state had become normal to others and didn't register.

Ewan and Gemma naturally took me in like family, feeding my stomach and allowing me to rest. Ewan would whip up his signature tomato and melted cheese on toasted bread. Followed by smoking his craftsmanship styled spliffs—a joint with half tobacco—and many cups of tea with milk and sugar. I never shared with them anything about the clubbing or certainly not the park. I held it all inside, fearing rejection. Then the visits to Guildford became less frequent.

All along I kept my responsibility to The Magical Tour Company as it cast its spell on me. Patrick allowed me to assist him on two weekend tours. One brought me back to nature in the green rolling hills of Wales on a horseback riding adventure. Another exposed me to the culture of Belgium visiting Brussels and Brugge. They were breaths of fresh air away from the clubs for a couple weeks. During the week Patrick continued to give me lists of schools to deliver fliers to and encouraged me to take my time.

"There's a great park that you can go through in between these two schools," he would say. Or "There's a nice pub right outside the Underground station to stop for a Guinness."

So I would sit in the park, enjoy the autumn weather, and breathe in the crisp air. Or stop for the Guinness, which filled me up and became my lunch. All the walking kept me moving, stimulated, and outside seeing new places around London. I wanted to do a good job for Patrick and help promote his business. Pride was felt when I made it to all the schools on his list each day. It was a sense of accomplishment. I had purpose for that day.

At the same time I evolved into a Londoner. I would carry my umbrella everywhere, always prepared for the eventual rain. I also learned to speak the Underground language. I knew the different lines and stops from all my time spent on it and was able to give directions to others. The challenge of being in a new place, adapting and learning the ways, helped to keep me occupied from my issues.

It was during the weekend in Wales that I met Tripp and Julie, two friendly and easygoing Australians. They came to England on one-year working visas and lived in Notting Hill. We connected from the first stop for lunch along the tour after visiting Chepstow, the oldest castle in Wales. Tripp and Julie approached my table for conversation over a pint of beer. I was sitting alone being the only single guy on the tour.

Tripp was 5'10" and built stocky like a rugby player. He had reddish brown hair, brown eyes and rugged looks. From the outside he looked like someone not to upset. But when he opened his mouth or smiled a gentle and friendly demeanor exuded.

Julie was a few inches shorter then Tripp. Her hair was long and dirty blond with much of it resting in front of each shoulder while the bangs stretched to her blue eyes. She was a bit more reserved in the beginning. Demure. But as we talked she opened up like a beautiful flower blooming.

They were kind-of-a-couple—their time in England a sort of testing ground for their feelings. Tripp however seemed more certain in his affections for Julie. He was very protective and doting toward her, the type of guy that wanted to look out for his friends. He was a catch.

They were open to new friends for new adventures, which was equally reciprocated by me. I was intrigued also by the fact they were from another country as the majority of people on the tour were American. So it was very easy for me to give them an abridged story of Joe and how I came to be in England.

By the end of the pint we had bonded, realizing we were fellow travelers yearning to experience whatever lied ahead. The meeting made the trip more exciting with the presence of other like-minded individuals. Whether we ever saw each other again or not, Wales was *our* time together.

The next day we arrived at the ranch in the Brecon Beacons National Park. We picked up our horses that would lead us on our journey through the expansive, rolling green—and wet—hills of Wales. It was a typically rainy, dreary, and cold autumn day for Wales. As we donned our ponchos to protect us from whatever wetness they would, the group followed our guide into the country in a single file line. Tripp, Julie and I brought up the rear.

When the wind began to blow and the rain continued in a steady pour, much of the group complained about being wet and cold. But through our hoods the three of us connected with glances, laughs, and a bigger picture.

I *was* very cold. Even more so each second as the tips of my toes and fingers began to numb. But I tried to look around at the beautiful green hills, rising and falling into each other, while the train of horses strolled along the trail. It was a part of nature at its best, rain and all.

When else will I ever be in the hills of Wales on a horse? I thought to myself. *Probably never. So be here now Jason. Because* now *is the time for this particular experience in life.*

It helped to separate myself from my cold and wet body. I sensed from Tripp and Julie's laughs and smiles they felt the same. Bonding us further.

That night our bus invaded a small, Welsh village. We stayed at the lone hotel. It was also the only place to be for a "big" Saturday night of dancing. After drinking a few pints at the local pub the group moved back to the hotel.

We then multiplied the village's energy with our animated attitude. It gave the villagers an international taste of some amusing foreigners. The expressions on some of the locals' faces mixed surprised surrealism with joyful thrill as we sang and danced to the present hits in the UK.

One of which was Sonique's "Sky". Tripp, Julie and I began singing along as loud as we could while dancing as if no one was watching. The lyrics acted as a prophecy from deep inside, trying to come out and reach me:

Follow me
To a place where we can be
Absolutely free
To be exactly what you want to be

At the night's end Tripp and Julie invited me to their room to share a joint. As we smoked and recapped the night's events our abs ached from laughter.

"Did you see how everyone in the group completely let loose tonight?" Julie said.

"Yeah we really saw a different side of everyone. A side that didn't care what anybody thought. That just wanted to have fun!" Tripp added.

"And the looks on some of the villagers' faces! Absolutely priceless!" I said as we all started laughing.

"It was magical," Julie said. "Like a bunch of gypsies putting on a show. Casting a spell setting good vibrations and entertainment into the air."

"Well said!" Tripp and I simultaneously said then looked at each other surprised we were in sync with our thoughts. Then we continued laughing along with Julie.

"It was like a mini version of a night clubbing in London," I said.

"Is that what clubbing is like in the city?" Tripp asked.

I looked at him with a confused expression.

"How long have you guys been in England again?" I asked.

"Nine months," Julie answered.

"Nine months! And you haven't experienced London's club scene?" I asked shocked.

"No," they both said.

"London clubs are known for being some of, if not *the* best in the world," I replied. "Give me your mobile numbers, or emails or *something* to get a hold of you by." Julie found a piece of paper and pen and began writing their details down. "When we get back I'm going to take you both out for a proper night in London! You simply can't go back to Australia until you've had one!"

"Sounds great mate," Tripp said. "We'd both love that!" Julie nodded in agreement. We hugged and retired for the night. The next morning we boarded the bus back to London for the start of another workweek.

As time went on, I tried to maintain my working and clubbing routine. But my body became fatigued. With the weather growing colder outside, all the miles of walking each week and the late nights clubbing, I became sick and missed days of work. The money I allotted for London was disappearing. I had not connected again with Joe. All of it combined with the dueling lives made it more arctic and darker inside. Everything felt so heavy on my mind, my body, and my heart. I didn't care what happened anymore. And was tired of choosing my own adventure.

Then one morning during rush hour I was making my way through the herd of people. As I walked down the corridor toward my platform I began to hear music floating through the air. It sounded familiar. Then a busker began to sing.

"I see trees of green . . . red roses too . . . I see them all . . . for me and you . . . and I think to myself . . . what a wonderful world . . ."

My heart stopped, and I thought of Joe. I remembered the tape of his I found shortly after his death with the same song. For a brief moment my heart felt lighter as I welcomed in the words. And it brought me through one more day.

Then at night as I exited Baker Street station to go home I passed the homeless sitting in the tunnel underneath the street. I gave whatever change was in my pocket. I didn't want *anything.* Not the money. Not acknowledgement. Their tattered and dirty appearance on the outside reflected my inside. I just wanted to rid myself of everything in my world. Including my existence.

I usually tried to avoid their eyes so I would not have to receive a "thank you", *especially* from their eyes. But one evening, for the first time my eyes accidently met a homeless man's as I stopped to drop my change. There was such pure gratitude shining from his eyes. It struck me. Stunned me, as it penetrated deeply through the vault. And suspended my fall.

When Thanksgiving arrived The Americans and I celebrated together as foreigners bound by a mutual tradition. Before I met them at the restaurant I stopped in a red phone booth to call my family. After being passed to everyone the phone reached my mother.

"Did you get my card? Is there somewhere you can cash the check I sent?" she asked.

"Yes, thank you," I replied.

"Good, then take yourself out for a nice dinner," she said.

"I am," I said.

"I received your bank statement as well. There's nothing left," she continued.

Her words were unexpected. According to my records I thought I had enough for the remaining two weeks in London. After which I had a small reserve of traveler's checks to aid as seed money to start my life in Europe. Exchange fees and rates must have been overlooked or miscalculated.

"Ok," I replied a bit frozen. Immediately trying to come up with a new plan.

"Are you going to be okay?" she asked.

"Yes, yes, do not worry," I replied. "I will be alright." How, I did not know. But somehow trusted I would.

I hung up the phone then stood in the booth absorbing my new situation. In that moment I figured there were two choices. I could worry what the future held. Or I could be in the moment. I had money for the holiday dinner. Which signified gratefulness and giving thanks. Plus people to share it with and celebrate. I chose the latter.

I met up with The Americans at a crowded restaurant in our neighborhood. It offered an American style Thanksgiving meal in a chic European design. All the traditional foods were neatly stacked upon one another for an elegant presentation.

For those few hours I immersed myself and concentrated only on the moment. And the people I shared it with. Escaping into them in a good way. I finally learned about them, beyond the surface; what their families were like, what their Thanksgiving traditions were, stories of past holidays and childhood. There were cheers. Smiles. And laughter.

I was still too guarded to speak of Joe. With such a celebratory setting I felt it would bring the mood down to mention death. I assumed they would not want to hear about it. But we all had a good time together as I began to see them as individuals. They were all a good mix and representation from the different areas they came. But more importantly genuinely *good* people as I started to learn.

The next day I woke with determination to keep whatever life I had going. I traveled to a shop in Notting Hill I discovered that bought and sold old clothes. I'd packed extra professional attire for the conventional internship I believed it would be that I never used. So I sold them. I also sold my favorite three-quarter length, thick black leather jacket that felt like a warm blanket wrapped around me. Of everything I had I knew it would get the most money. I was left with a light, black insulated vest as winter approached.

Although I spent much of the new money clubbing it was different than previous weekends. I went to Fabric that night with Miles. The same club Ewan, Gemma and I visited when I had the spiritual experience with Joe. It had become my home club because it had special meaning to me through Ewan and Gemma. But also because The Americans were naturally drawn to it as well since it brought in some of the best DJs and spun the music we wanted to hear.

Up to that point Miles exuded a tough Jewish guy from the Bronx exterior although he was in fact very polite and nice, always checking in with me each week before making the ecstasy runs for the flat. He had not revealed too much about himself throughout the semester. But neither had I.

Miles had thick curly black hair and a fit body with dark eyes and stood at 5'10". He exemplified the cool kid you hoped would be your friend. Or at least knew you existed in high school. He looked and acted suave and emanated self-confidence.

From the beginning Miles constantly played Drum & Bass music throughout the flat. I had never heard it before and didn't understand it. I found it loud and fast with too much going on. But throughout the semester he took the time to share his passion for it while we attended Drum & Bass nights on Fridays at Fabric.

His rapture for the music shined brilliantly when he danced to it. He embodied every note and beat, becoming the perfect poster boy. I was hooked watching him like an eager student trying to learn some of his moves. He was like lightning, electrifying in all directions that he moved as he escaped into and became one with the music.

In a quiet upper level area of the club that night, away from the mass of people, we sat on a couch to take a break from dancing. We were smoking, but not speaking. Simply taking in the music. Finally the urge to know more about the person sitting next to me—that I had been sharing a home with—bubbled out.

"Tell me something about yourself that none of the other guys know," I said. I was a bit nervous to ask him a deeper question, to penetrate the tough guy persona.

"Like what?" he asked.

"Anything, whatever you want to share," I said.

"Well, my sister has diabetes and it has been scary at times for my family with a couple of close calls," he said. I didn't expect the *cool* kid to share something like that. But felt excited that he opened up to me.

"How did it make you feel?" I asked.

"It's hard to watch her go through it sometimes, but my family has always just kind of done what has needed to be done to stay strong and supportive for her."

"Wow, that's great," I said. "Sounds like you and your family are very close."

"Yeah we are," he said. "What about you? Tell me something that none of the other guys know." I hesitated for a moment. I wanted to share about Joe but was fearful.

"Well, I have three brothers. But one of them died in a car accident about three years ago," I finally said.

"Sorry to hear. What was he like?" he responded.

"He was a dancer, a very good one. Mostly modern but some ballet," I said.

"Sounds like he was very talented," he said.

"He was," I replied. As I continued to share more I felt lighter inside. It was a feeling different from the effects of the drugs. I felt the heaviness in my heart and mind lift.

The following night the whole household went out together. I approached the others one by one the same way I did with Miles in sharing Joe. Like Miles they were all kind and compassionate. Their listening and acceptance gave more depth and dimension to the characters they were.

Tim and Josh both exemplified wholesome Midwestern values. Tim was in the military and his physique showed it. His posture was straight and he had a body packed and toned with tight muscles. He was reserved and manly in his demeanor during the day from his military training with very strong handshakes. But he also had a wild polar opposite night persona, which was amplified with music and dancing. He would let loose and get pumped up like Animal from The Muppets. But more in an entertaining and hilariously endearing way—like a Jester—juxtaposed to his military background than a bad boy party animal.

Josh had a more stocky build with dirty blond hair and facial scruff and wore small wire rimmed glasses. He loved to write and was a movie buff that dreamed of writing a screenplay. He would often recite his favorite lines from movies when they applied to the conversation at hand,

and these usually produced laughter from all, including himself, as his silly side shined through.

And Nathan, who towered over all of us at 6'3", had a lanky body that seemed all arms and legs. His hair was buzzed and dark brown. He would assist or help any of us in an instant, an enormous giver with a big heart. Nathan was well traveled and exposed to many of the differences in life and people. He exhibited the awareness and acceptance of life's beauty and diversity. He sometimes disappeared for hours, even days, and upon his return usually had a crazy story relaying the mishaps of his mini-adventures around the city.

It was after that weekend that our flat felt more like our home. We began to nest together there more often. Especially after nights out clubbing, always hoping to get home before the sun came up. We were like silly little harmless vampires scurrying through the streets to get inside to the warmth and close all the shades. Then we'd grab the duvets off our beds and wrap them around us as we gathered in the living room to share the stories of the night. Our choice of blood was traditional English Breakfast tea that I would maternally make for everyone. They usually requested it "just like yours", with a little milk and sugar. Except for Miles who was unique in his choice, just as he was, with peppermint tea, no milk or sugar.

Afterward we'd drift off to sleep—usually to the sounds of jazz musician Donald Byrd's CD *Electric Byrd* echoing throughout the flat. It was a favorite of Miles that he introduced to the rest of us. The hallucinating sounds provided a magic carpet that carried us off to dreamland.

Muhammad's lesson about the culture of Egypt sharing so that no one went without manifested in our London home. Whatever any one lacked when we went out and another had, we shared; food, cigarettes, pills or money. The overall goal was to ensure everyone had a good time *together*. My emotional and mental health greatly improved.

The following week there was a German-style Christmas festival with booths of different crafts in Covent Garden. I felt happier, gently peeking into life again, like a scared child from underneath the covers. I wanted to share it in some way with my family and send them Christmas gifts from England.

Tim, Josh and I went to the festival together. It was four o'clock in the afternoon on a Sunday a few weeks before Christmas as early winter darkness approached. There were hundreds of people walking around.

Some Chinese buskers playing instruments were set up outside the Underground station as we exited. Tim and Josh went in one direction, while I went to shop for gifts. We planned to meet an hour later.

As I wandered in and out of the different booths I thought of each member of my family. If something reminded me of someone I bought it. One by one I spent time with them in my mind and heart imagining them opening the gifts. I wanted the gifts to be special. It would be my first Christmas away from them.

As I walked over to the entrance of the station where I was to meet Tim and Josh I came upon the Chinese performers. Just as I did they were beginning a new song. It was the song from *Titanic*, "My Heart Will Go On", the same one I heard as I approached Joe's grave for the first time on his birthday.

I smiled as I thought of Joe and paused to listen. As I carried on afterward through the crowd of people I felt my head turn to the right. There was no one I knew there but I felt a strong presence walking beside me. I was spooked with chills even underneath my many layers. *Poof!* It was Joe.

I doubted it and looked to my left. There was no one there and I did not feel any presence. I looked and felt one more time to my right. The presence was still there. He was not a missing piece through death anymore. I was with my family in mind and heart and he found a way to be there as well. And let me know.

"There you are," I whispered to him. "You scared me. I've been looking for you. It's about time you came to visit."

It was like an explosion of fireworks inside from the love and connection I felt. As the spark's heat sublimated the dry ice vault it finally freed me. Until nothing remained but a man that did not have to go through death's door. Not yet at least. Initially death felt trapping in the vault, forever cold. But with time it changed forms—like Joe—as I went through death to its other side where life lived again. And learned to live with it and respect it as part of life. Joe had been with me all along. Surrounding me. Being with me as I learned to live again.

The experience made me feel sane. I wasn't on any drugs this time. I could not prove what I felt. But the time with family and the connection to the song at that moment was proof enough for me. Joe was okay and with me all along the way. It raised my hope for life again as the darkness faded, along with my anger toward America.

For the remaining weeks in London I felt completely in the present taking on the experience as it came. I felt uplifted. I wanted to celebrate. My aspirations for my career got pushed to the side. London held a different purpose, which felt achieved. I sensed my time in London was complete. I didn't know what was going to happen. All that mattered was concentrating on happiness and reveling for a moment atop the mountain of accomplishment I felt I had ascended. Thoughts of dealing with my sexuality pushed aside, for that moment I was happy to have life.

Not long before I left I made good on my promise to take Tripp and Julie out for a proper London club experience. I wanted to share with them Fabric, where so many great nights with all the others took place. But when we arrived it was not happening.

We had already popped our pills so we quickly found a convenience store and flipped through a *TimeOut* magazine for other clubs in the area. There was one called 333 nearby that we all considered a perfect sign for the *three* of us. With giggles burping out as the pills began to peak we dashed inside.

The music and energy was at its maximum. We quickly made our way to the dance floor, rarely leaving aside to get water. The experience in Wales had exponentially multiplied with a few hundred more people and music by some of the best DJs around. I could tell by their faces they had tasted a Dom Perignon with filet mignon experience of London.

"Mate," Tripp began as we strolled the streets after in the early morning hours, "we both want to thank you for an amazing night."

"Really, Jason," Julie added, "we had such a good time and couldn't imagine our time in England being complete without this experience. The music, the dancing, and especially the company were all spot-on for the night!"

"No worries," I said. "Welcome to the world I've been living in for the past few months. It's not that big of deal. I'm happy to have been able to share it with you both. It really was my pleasure."

"Well it is a big deal to us, mate," Tripp continued with genuine sincerity in his eyes. "Julie and I were talking before we left the club as you were getting our coats, and well, we'd really love it if you continued your travels after Europe on down under. Come visit us in our country and allow us to repay the hospitality you've shown us."

"Please say yes," Julie quickly added. "You don't have to worry about accommodation because you have us."

"Wow," I began. "That's a really generous offer. I have begun to feel my adventure in Europe coming to a close, which has surprised me because I set out to start a life here. I had not given much thought to what would be next."

"Then just say you'll come," Tripp said. "Choose Australia as your next adventure!"

"Well," I began then paused. "All I can think of to say is . . ." I hesitated for a moment more to build the suspense as I started to smile big. "Why not!?" We all hugged and started laughing then began making our way home before the sun came up.

When I returned home I climbed into bed. The feelings of ecstasy and bliss remained strong in my body from the large doses of serotonin released from my brain. As I waited for the effects of the drug to wear off and the Tylenol PM to kick in, my thoughts drifted to my parents.

First I thought of a man in his late twenties—not much older than myself—returning from Vietnam. Taking classes. Trying to build a life and future for himself.

Then I thought of a woman, also in her late twenties, who loved children. And chose to be a nurse, to take care of the newborns, while dreaming of children of her own one day.

These two people were set up on a blind date by the man's aunt, also a nurse, who worked with the woman. She believed they would make a good match. I imagined them dating, getting to know each other, discussing dreams for their life and of creating a family. I envisioned them falling in love and getting engaged three months later. And all the happiness the decision of making a commitment to each other brought. Then I thought of a wedding full of family and friends and love and a little apartment together. Their first *home.*

Then my heart celebrated for the young couple when they had their first child ten months later. The joys that must have filled their home and grew their love after creating a baby who was a little bit of each of them. Watching with excitement all the firsts that the baby would experience. Learning how to care for the marvelous little creature.

A few years later I imagined the family grow with a second child's arrival. And move into their first house together. Then only fifteen months later another child entered the family. As I thought of all the excitement that three small boys and the whirlwind adventure that creating and having a family must have brought the young couple, my heart filled with joy for them.

I imagined them watch and guide each son through all the ups and downs, joys, sorrows, and accomplishments of childhood: broken limbs; learning to speak; being afraid of the dark and boogey monsters; new discoveries and experiences with foods, school, making friends, creating art and riding bicycles.

Then seven years after the third child they discovered they would have a fourth. I imagined their concern for the woman, who was older, at being pregnant. They prayed every day until the birth of the child, that he would be healthy. The couple expressed excitement to the other children, explaining to them about life as they watched their new sibling and their mother's tummy grow.

During that time the couple experienced the full cycle of life, losing her father. They leaned on each other, becoming a stronger family unit, and explained to their children about death.

When the fourth child was born, the new life brought tremendous joy in the home. The older children learned about a baby and were able to experience all of his firsts.

The couple then built their own dream home with the love and desire to provide their children with the best experience they could. One filled with stability, opportunity and promise. And one that showed them they were all a part of it by letting them pick out their own room and décor, giving them their own haven.

With the family and home complete I imagined what it must have felt like for the couple to now settle down into it and enjoy the remaining years as a family living together before they set their children out into the world. And my heart filled with even more joy for them to the point of bursting.

Year by year, school dance to school dance, graduation to graduation, I went through in my mind. My love for the couple grew for all that they achieved. I felt as close as I could, without having children of my own, of walking alongside them, coming to fully appreciate and genuinely be in awe of what a truly tremendous feat they accomplished.

Then I imagined them receiving sudden, shocking news that one of their children was dead. And then, I could no longer imagine. My already closed eyes squeezed tighter as darkness blanketed everything and a huge abyss opened up in my thoughts.

And at the edge of that abyss was where my journey with the couple ended. I did not have to go into the abyss—neither in my thoughts, nor in my reality. It was not an exploration for this explorer to embark upon. But the couple did, together, go into the abyss. And they are the only two alive that know *that* particular journey. All I could do as I drifted off to sleep was make a decision to love them more deeply than ever before. And try to take care of myself so that they would never have to experience that again. Choose life no matter what.

On my last night in London, Tim, Miles, and I went to The Fridge, a club in Brixton, south London. I left the dance floor to find a place to sit down. It was crowded and I sat between two people. When I turned to my right a slender man in his mid-twenties with a shaved head was gazing at me with a starry calm look of wonder in his eyes. I felt a bit shy the way he intently examined me. Through me. Into me.

"Ciao," he said with a seductive Italian accent. "I am Fabio, from Florence."

"Hi," I said, "I'm Jason."

"If you were a flower," he began, "what would you be?"

The question was so random that it took me by complete surprise. It made me a bit nervous. As if a spotlight was shining down upon me.

"I don't know," I replied. "What would you be?"

Then with the passion of a poet he responded, "I would be a sunflower. For they stretch and reach for all the light and warmth of the sun so that they can continue to grow and grow!"

"I like that," I said. "I would be a sunflower too."

9

I was running late to catch my train the mid-December morning I departed London. As I rushed to get ready I passed by the hall mirror and caught a surprising glimpse. I dropped my bags and went back for another look. In my reflection I saw a gaunt skeleton of a man. The transformation seemed so all of the sudden to me.

But then I looked into my eyes and noted fresh sparkle. I felt hunger and excitement for life again. So I was not that concerned with my thinner appearance. I quickly grabbed my bags and flew out the door to my underground stop at Baker Street for the last time as a Londoner.

The Eurostar departed from Waterloo Station, gliding me out of my London womb through the Chunnel, a new, more modern birthing canal. I had one month left in Europe and I wondered where—and how—I would call home with what little money I had left, just a few hundred dollars.

But the feeling of bliss for life and the belief in everything working out ran so high I surrendered the situation. I trusted if I made it that far a door would open. I concentrated my thoughts on being grateful for that home, wherever it was, as the train pulled into Central Station and delivered me to Amsterdam. Our fourth date.

Amsterdam and I were brought together again after London to meet Dallas. The timing couldn't have been more perfect to reunite with an old friend. Although it was to be a brief visit it was going to be a celebration.

And Dallas was the appropriate person. He was there for me in the beginning of life without Joe. And now for the third time he was meeting me in Europe, grounding me at what I felt was a positive rebirth through the darkness from it all.

Dallas's brother Max was studying abroad in Leiden, a town just outside of Amsterdam, so he came to visit us both. Once reunited, I shared the London experience with them, sans my hideouts in Hyde. I didn't embrace that part of the rebirth was into a gay life as to me that was still another person. I also shared my dilemma of no current home or much funds for one. Fortunately Max kindly offered me his dorm while he visited America for the holidays.

After Dallas left, Max finished up his finals and gave me a crash course of life in The Netherlands. We would ride around on his bike, me balancing on the back Dutch style, as he helped me learn my way around Leiden; where the market was, what days it was open, how to get to the train station and a bit of Dutch: "please" and "thank you", the bare minimum when visiting another country.

Once Max returned to America I was left with my own home in Holland. Growing up I had the influence of the Polish culture through food, dance, and bits of language surrounding me on both sides of my family. Now I had the opportunity to live in and truly experience the land of my Dutch ancestors through my paternal grandmother. It was a unique door into my past that I gratefully and happily stepped through. I developed a routine during my three weeks. My job I gave myself was to explore different areas to gain a feel of the country, enjoying one place and experiencing it as a local. I did day trips to Den Haag, Rotterdam, and Zondvoort an Zee. But most of the time I took the train to Amsterdam, where I remained a student, taking a new course: My Sexuality 101.

I usually arrived at Central Station in the late afternoon or early evening. I would begin in the southwest part of the city at Leidseplein Square. One of the crossroads of the square is Leidsestraat, which was originally named for being the road to Leiden. Historically the square was the end of the road from Leiden. With my home in Leiden, never knowing the connection, I was naturally drawn to start a new road from it.

I fell in love with the square. Its energy was so vibrant and alive. There were always street performers and live music. One such performer was Soccer Man, whom I had seen since my first date with Amsterdam and every time since. I always stopped to observe his amazing abilities. He would sit somewhere on the square and bounce a soccer ball from one foot to the next over and over while doing tricks. He rarely ever dropped the ball. Sometimes he would climb one of the lampposts that surround the square and hang from it while continuing to bounce the ball from each foot. He always drew a crowd. Sometimes if I was lucky he would shoot me a smile, acknowledging my presence. The shine from his eyes made it a more personal and intimate experience as he drew me in with a sense of captivating magic for more.

A violinist's notes would float through the crisp winter air as the lights strung around the trees created an ethereal ambiance. There were people on bikes, or with children or animals, that along with the tram making its appearance every few minutes, added to the eclectic scene. The city was electrified with life, reflecting what I felt. I had renewed breath in my body and was incredibly humbled to experience it.

But as much as I was in love with life, I was not in love with myself. I felt in touch with my soul but still not with my identity as Jason. Nevertheless a spell of love was in the air.

I had three weeks left in Europe and was nearly broke. But I was in the original "Gay Capitol of Europe" with a happy state of mind for exploration. It was like being a kid in a candy store and the variety of bonbon were sexy. But I never considered that to some of them I too was candy.

I would often start my exploration with a warm cup of tea and a joint at a coffeeshop near the square called De Rokerij. It had become a favorite over previous visits to Amsterdam. It had a relaxed atmosphere with dim lighting and Indian style décor. In the back were wooden benches and small stools creating different seating areas that were covered in colorful pillows. A large mandala filled with colors was painted on one wall while an image of two elephants facing each other was painted on the opposite wall. Above there were ceiling fans that were set to extreme slow motion, which added to the tranquil mood. The coffee shop was a great place to sit down next to a stranger and strike up a conversation or just listen to the music. It became a living room in my Amsterdam home to relax or do some writing

As evening turned into night my journey flowed to the bars. Usually the cold would get to me before I arrived. So I would take cover at the entrance of a store, stand on its edge between the warmth and cold to soak up the heat for a few moments, before heading back into the street.

Soon I would be upon Reguilerswarsstraat. It was lined with many gay bars, including Havana's. Havana's was always very lively, loud, and full of people. It made it easy for me to slip in and simply observe. The bar itself was round and in the center of the venue with large open spaces around it.

I was too shy to introduce myself to anyone. If anyone talked to me or bought me a drink I politely yet briefly thanked them, then quickly excused myself to find some place to sit down. Alone.

In the back were stairs that led up to a small balcony, which overlooked the main floor. It was wide enough to fit two small round tables. The one most secluded in the corner was a perfect spot to tuck away and be a wallflower.

One evening I was sitting upon my balcony like Juliet. There were many people buzzing around below. The music was upbeat and sparkling. People were talking, laughing and dancing amongst one another. Except one.

I noticed a single man standing in the middle of the floor. His posture was straight and he stood 5'9". He had a lean runner's build. His hands were relaxed at his side, not fidgeting or holding onto anything. While he scanned the room, he had a slight smile on his face. He wore a blue knit cap pulled to the top of his eyes. Blond hair peeked out from underneath. His winter coat was slightly big on him and hung down below his waist. He stood out because he too was alone. I felt a bold yet gentle confidence emanating from him. As if it spoke, "*Here* I am."

I was immediately captivated. He appeared happy and able to enjoy his own company, his head moving in rhythm with the music. He was in the moment, absorbing it all. His smile remained the entire time. Everywhere he looked. Everywhere, but up.

As he shifted to face another direction his body seemed to glide. But his presence stayed grounded. His feet firmly planted. He stood there for quite some time. Not talking to anyone. He was magnetic. I could not take my eyes off him. I thought to myself, *If there's anyone in the bar I would like to get to know, it's* him.

But I was still too excruciatingly shy. Eventually, he moved on. I felt disappointed at my inability to interact as the opportunity passed me by.

After the bars began to close I moved on to the clubs. They were on Warrmoustraat, another gay area near the train station. Many of the clubs did not have signs distinguishing them, but I could tell where they were as the men entered and exited. But one very much stood out—Cockring.

Cockring was spelled out in bold capital letters. Each metal letter connected by rods protruded from a black wall. There was a large ring around the "K" and "R" at a diagonal angle, which completed the three-dimensional feel. The venue was a bit intimidating but curiosity percolated as to what was behind its black walls. Somehow I felt by going in I would not be simply tasting that world, but fully biting into it like a lion into flesh. It provided a personal challenge.

The first time I entered it was just after midnight. First I walked up and down the street passing it several times. Then, as if I was about to break through an imaginary wall into another realm, my step gained speed and I quickly turned toward the door.

The door was cut in two. Only the top half was open. A tall, muscular doorman stood behind the closed lower half. He saw me approach and as I stepped up the gate opened.

I checked my bag and coat then went down a flight of stairs and pushed through two doors that led to the lower level. There was a small bar to the left with an area to drink and mingle. Further ahead stepped down onto the dance floor. The mood was erotic but there weren't many people around. As I soon learned the clubs did not begin to fill up until after one. I walked to the other side of the dance floor. A DJ booth was to the left with another area to stand and drink. Or cruise. Or be cruised. At the end there was another staircase going up to the left. I ascended it to continue exploring the club.

About halfway up it turned left, then led up to a small landing with toilets to the left. Off the bathroom's entrance was another dark narrow staircase that winded up, leading *somewhere* . . . But I continued forward on the stairs I was already on. They led to a second bar with raised benches against the wall. Several television sets hung in the different corners playing gay porn. The volume turned low. Aside from the barman there were only a couple of people present.

Then my peeping drew me back to the staircase near the toilet. It was steep and each step narrow. It made a slight curve as I went up. I found myself in a dark room with two separate areas on either side of the entrance. There was only a small bit of light filtering in the room from the stairs. Another staircase that led back down into the bar was located on the opposite side. It had a door that blended in with the bar giving it a "secret" entrance or exit effect. Nobody was up there, so I took the secret staircase down. From there I descended a final staircase on the opposite side of the bar that led to the entrance. I collected my coat and bag and exited.

As I left I passed a man with a Mediterranean appearance. Dark hair and a V-shaped build. We glanced at each other as we passed on the street.

Then both looked back and paused for a moment. He stared for a lingering second before entering Cockring. I continued walking, but then stopped, turned around and went back inside.

I found him next sitting at the bar upstairs. He noticed me as I came up the stairs from the dance floor. We made eye contact. I stood near the entrance of the upstairs bar then took a seat on the bench against the wall.

He got up and walked toward me, long glancing at me as he passed. I watched him walk down the stairs to the next level then turn right toward the toilet. I followed.

I didn't see him in the bathroom so I went up the staircase to the dark room. At first I thought it was still empty but then I sensed him near the back corner of the room to my right. I slowly approached until I was standing right in front of him. Gradually I went in and we began kissing.

It was passionate, erotic and sensual. Our hands began to explore each other's body and slide up underneath each other's clothes. Then down to undo and lower the other's pants. He took my cock in his hand and placed it between his hairy thighs. Then closed them, alluding I enter him.

"Do you have a condom?" I asked.

"No," he replied.

I remembered I had a condom in my bag *way* downstairs. But I feared leaving would ruin the mood. So we continued to kiss. Still he pursued his mission to get me in. My desire to be inside him, safely, overcame.

"Wait here," I said. "I have a condom in my bag."

"Alright," he replied.

I bolted down the two flights of stairs, jumping two and three at a time. Then with speed to my walk scurried across the dance floor and pushed through the doors. I went up the stairs and handed the man at the coat check my number.

"I just need to get something out of my bag," I said. I felt sneaky, like a kid doing something wrong. He looked at me perceptively. Like I wasn't fooling him. Knowing it was drugs, a condom, sex toy, or some other accessory for a gay man's night of fun. Then he shot me a look like it didn't matter, turning a blind eye.

I grabbed the condoms and raced back to the dark room like a competing Olympian. After slipping the condom on, I entered him. I fucked him as we kissed. Then turned him around. He placed his hands on the wall like a convict caught by the police. I re-entered him while I wrapped one hand around his fur covered chest and the other around his stomach. Then thrust until we both came. From that night on I always made sure I had condoms on me *before* I checked my coat.

I followed him back down the stairs. We sat at the bar and he bought me a drink. He was Greek, just visiting Amsterdam. I really wanted to leave with him, to be alone and explore more the sensuality of being with a man. Privately. But he was not keen on leaving. I felt rejected and eventually left him sitting there.

Soon the club filled with men. I stayed, to take in more of the experience. I left around five in the morning and took the train back home to Leiden. Leidseplein to Cockring became my routine during my studies of my sexuality at the school of Amsterdam.

My interest in the dark room wasn't only for sex. It was a time and place where I could explore simply *being* with a man. And the dark room provided such an environment. It felt like meeting someone on another level or realm. Because I could not clearly see their human form, a sixth sense took the place of sight. It was simply a different approach to learning about someone, how that person felt, and what we felt together. Energetically. A heightened sensitivity developed in knowing if it was just sex. Or if it could be something more to bring out of the dark and discover if a compatibility existed.

But I was not ready or secure in myself to come out into the light. Just to physically connect with a man was my first step toward feeling comfortable. It felt essential before I could think of talking with someone. It was my way of making sure that man was what I really wanted. Before I came out of the dark.

Shame's dictator tried to enter. But the darkness helped me to hide from him as well. But when he found his way in, my heart would fight like someone who had been patient and good for so long finally speaking up for himself that he wanted men. And would lead me back for more, night after night.

On one particular evening I was sitting on a bench on the edge of the square before beginning my routine. In the center of the square I noticed a star in a circle surrounded by brick. I had stood on different spots in the square to look around and take in all the magic, except there.

But there was a boy bundled up in a leather jacket—reminiscent to the one I sold—and a black knit hat standing on the star. He looked warm and strong. I sat there with my arms—covered in a thermal shirt—crossed over my chest trying to keep my body heat from escaping my vest.

I became very intrigued about that particular spot. I wanted to experience the view of life from its perspective. So I waited for the boy to move. But he stayed for quite awhile. The longer he remained the more captivated I became, making me mentally drool at the thought of standing on the star.

Eventually he took a step off. Paused for a moment. Then took another look around. Smiling all the while and carried on into the night.

I sprung off the bench and hurried to the star to claim it. I loved standing on the star in the center of the square. It became my favorite spot on earth. My grounding point and reset button, my home base in the universe. With all the gypsy moves I had done that one spot in the world I adopted as mine. Finally after absorbing life from the view of the star, I took a step off eager to see what surprises and fun lied ahead in the enchantment of the night.

I made my way to the coffee shops and bars as usual and later from one to five wandered once again onto Waarmoustraat. There were bars there that I had not been into. Ones that still intimidated me like Cockring in the beginning. But I was feeling brave. The explorer in me wanted my eyes to see and experience something new.

There was one bar with a very small placard across the top of the door that read Argos. The attire of the men I observed entering and leaving consisted of some type of leather vest or harness as well as leather or denim pants. Some men wore white T-shirts. Others didn't have a shirt on at all underneath their vest or coat. Most also had some type of facial hair or scruff. It was a new type of scene in the gay world that I had not really been exposed to but was up for discovering.

I knocked. A hairy and stocky man with jeans, a black leather vest, and police officer style hat opened the door. He looked me up and down and simply said "Hoi" as the door opened wider for me to walk through.

The place inside was long and narrow, and very crowded. There was only a small path in the middle of all the men to walk through. Most eyes turned to notice the new meat that just entered. Me.

I felt a bit apprehensive as I squeezed and brushed past some of the men, making contact as I made my way through the first section. The bar ran along the right side. Then there were a couple steps that led up to the next area.

It felt like a catwalk. But I was not the model, rather the piece of fashion, as men wondered if I would fit them. I tried not to make too much eye contact but stole looks here and there to see if I was interested in anyone. As I made my way to the back of the bar to investigate more of its layout I thought to myself, *There is not one man that I am attracted to.*

Then I saw a very tall man, leaning against the wall. A light from the ceiling shined down on him like a spotlight. He was well built with muscles bulging under an army green tank top with a red star in the center. He wore camouflage pants and a black knit cap with bits of black hair peeking out. His face was chiseled with a strong jaw line.

If I were to choose someone in the bar I'm attracted to it would be him.

I glanced in his direction and he in mine. But I still refrained from making lingering eye contact with anyone. I was simply interested in exploring the rest of the bar. There was a black corkscrew staircase that led down into what I assumed was a dark room. So the explorer in me continued as I spiraled down into the dark.

There were many men below, most of which were gathered around the bottom of the stairs and used the little light that shined to get a look at who came down. It was an area the size of a railroad car cut in half and placed side by side, with a wall dividing it into two. Small specs of light provided guidance into each side but then grew darker toward the back.

I checked out the area on the right first but did not go back too far. Then I returned and searched the one on my left. I was a little more adventuresome, going further in until I started to bump into people. Then I heard the sounds of pleasure and buckles clinking. And felt their heated breath. A few hands reached up to touch and feel me but I quickly turned and walked back toward the stairs.

I stood near the bottom of the stairs with a group of about six or seven men while I waited for some men who were descending. The stairs were not large enough for people to go up and down at the same time. One of the men I noticed as he squeezed through the group was the one I thought was attractive earlier.

Hmmm, let's just see where he is going . . .

I followed behind with a little distance between us. He entered the area on the right but he soon came back out of the darkness. Just as he passed a bit of light shining down, I gasped.

Oh my god, I thought. *He looks like Rupert Everett! No, that can't be him. Why would a movie star be here?!*

Then I deductively reasoned that it very well could be him. Number one, he *is* gay. Number two, I was in a gay bar. Number three, he is

European and was just in Scotland for Madonna's wedding because it was in all the papers shortly before I left London. So why wouldn't he have a little extended holiday in the gay capitol of Europe? It was like a mini movie adventure with me cast in a scene with Rupert Everett. The adventurer in me had to find out for sure if it was really Rupert or his stand-in.

I followed the man into the second area but did not fully enter. He briefly went to the back then returned toward the entrance and stood in the corner. Two men approached him and started touching him. He didn't pay them much attention before they attempted to go down on him.

I inched closer. Sex was the last thing on my mind. I simply wanted to know if it was really Rupert. I tried to examine his silhouette but he kept turning his head toward the stairs. I moved in for an even closer look, brushing against the two persistent men who were getting nowhere with their advances.

Then while star struck at the very idea it may be him, the mystery man's hand reached up and touched my right arm. He moved in closer, looking down at me in the dark, nudging the other pursuers out of the way. Then he began kissing me.

I returned the kiss without a second thought. He was an excellent kisser. Passionately he stuck his tongue in my mouth, penetrating it wildly, as if giving a prelude of what he could do with his cock. At the same time he was very sensual. His hand went up my shirt to my pectoral and nipple, then down to my pants, where he caressed my crotch. I put both hands all over him, exploring his muscular body from his arms and chest to his ass and every erect inch. All the while I kept repeating in my head, *I think I'm kissing Rupert Everett!*

Our lips locked for several minutes. *If this is really Rupert,* I thought, *he has worked with and kissed favorite stars of mine, like Madonna!* My potential one-degree of separation from their lips made me giggle inside. Then just as unexpectedly as the passion started, it stopped. He pulled away, zipped up his pants, and began making his way toward the stairs.

I quickly composed myself and also made my way back up stairs. I wanted to see him again with the better light of the bar area but I lost him when I reached the top of the staircase. I scurried my way to the front of the room, glancing around for him.

Then I noticed the man with the red star on his chest sitting against the wall on a bench. He was looking out toward nothing as someone attempted to speak to him. I took a good long look at his profile the entire time I walked to the door. Then, just before I exited, as if he knew I was there, he turned and looked me directly in the eye.

Yup, I'm 95 percent sure that's him, I thought. I gave a warm smile and a nod, as cool and collected as I could, before I made my exit stage right out the door.

As soon as I hit the street the excitement of the possibility made me squeal like a little kid. I jumped up and down for a few moments and laughed all the way to the train station. Regardless of the man's true identity, the shared experience was a baby boost of confidence as I continued to explore my sexuality.

That night I climbed into bed and turned on the TV. Flipping channels, I paused with pure joy when I saw none other than Madonna and Rupert Everett on the screen singing "American Pie". *Is it a sign confirming the other 5 percent?* I thought.

"If that *was* you Rupert, Thank you," I whispered as I watched them sing me to sleep.

Aside from the small stray to Argos that night and one or two other places explored, the majority of the bewitching hours were spent at Cockring. Its hypnotic Alpha male spell was cast with the first allure and challenge of even entering. It was magnetic the way it pulled me in each night. I felt safe there. Safe to explore from the outside world's judgments. It was a secure haven.

One evening there, in the dark room, I was drawn through all of the men to one. He simply allowed me to touch him all over. I ran my hands across his eyes, his lips, and down his arms to his hands where our fingers intertwined. Simply held. Then I gently kissed his cheeks, his eyes, his lips. I continued by lifting his shirt, brushing his nipples with my fingers, and running my hands down his bare back.

It began to get very hot and steamy in the small crowded room with all the body heat of the other men and the smell of their pheromones floating through the air. The boy wore a knit cap that I took off once I felt his body heat rise. I wiped away the drops of sweat that began to form on his head and ran my fingers through his hair.

There was something very grounding being there with him. He was so present in the moment happening. It was as if I could read his thoughts and they did not wander. *Anywhere* else.

And then I felt as if he were inside my thoughts. Which were of nothing but interest in him. Being with him. Touching him. So he remained for as long as was needed. Wanted. Forever, if that was the case.

I felt incredibly calm and at peace in his arms. Even being surrounded by all the other men and their primal desire around us. Sometimes a hand would reach in here or there in an attempt to join in, but I would push it away. My only interest was in exploring him.

As our dance became more symbiotic he followed by exploring my body. Pushing my shirt up and pressing our bare bodies together, just embracing, going slowly. We both moved our hands to each other's pants, caressing and unzipping. He went down on me, taking me in as I gently held his head with his sweaty hair moving through my fingers.

But I soon missed his kiss. And it was as if he knew, or he too missed mine, that he rose. And when he did I reached for a condom from my pocket and put it on as we began to kiss again. The foreplay grew into an equally erotic and passionate moment of sex as I entered him. Sensing and moving with each other's body like one.

Each night I went back to the dark room I would have a similar experience with a man that I began to sense was the same one. It always evolved to more than just sex, to include touching, kissing, and simply holding one another. Although we did equally become erotically curious to try different positions as much as two could in a crowd of men. I turned him around and put my arms through his, clutching his chest as my fingers reached, wrapping around his shoulders and held his body close as I entered him. Smelled him. Felt him.

The sole priority was the other's pleasure. I would gently breathe close to his skin, inhaling deeply and letting out a long, slow exhale on his neck, across his face. Blanketing him with my warmth as I felt his warm breath on me. All of the senses except sight were alive, breathing in and out together in unison—making love.

I would stare at him in the dark and feel his eyes staring back at me. I would try to sense what he looked like but would then get drawn back into feeling him and being with him. Gradually each time we met it was if we simply sensed and knew it was the other. Afterward, I felt vulnerable and would squeeze through the crowd and dash out the club before he could see me in the light.

Once the spell was cast I returned each night. And would see his silhouette glide through the crowd with a sense of eagerness and excitement that I was back. Standing in our usual spot, in the center. Waiting.

This went on for a number of earthly nights. But in each there was no beginning or end once together. It could have been an hour or two each night in the dark room but the whole period seems timeless because time ceased to exist.

Nothing on the surface mattered. Simply what it felt like to be together, like we were one. But we never said a word to one another. Not until the last night. It was just after Christmas, the 28th, after we had made love and were holding one another.

"What is your name?" he asked.

"Michael," I replied. I was still so insecure at the time to be Jason, a gay man.

"Where are you from?" he asked.

"I'm a student in London," I answered.

"When are you coming back to Amsterdam?"

"Not for a very long time," I replied. I was so shy to be speaking to a man I had been so intimate with that I could only give such short responses to his questions. I didn't even think to ask him any—not even his name.

And then he asked *the* question.

"Do you know what this is?" he said. I was so nervous with the question and didn't know the answer so there was a moment of silence. I did not say anything. Then very simply and directly with a confidence in his tone he replied. "This is love."

Still I didn't say anything. I didn't understand love between two men and most importantly I had no love for myself as a gay man. My soul knew he was right. But I had not learned how to listen to it.

We moved to another area of the room for a moment and then he guided me through the dark down the secret staircase that led to the bar. There on the stairs near the door we felt each other's presence for a little longer, caressing one another's skin. It was nice to be there alone on the staircase with him instead of surrounded by others.

"Do you have someplace we can go?" he asked.

"No," I replied. "Do you?"

I was too afraid to bring him back to Max's place. I felt if we went there it would combine my two lives and I wasn't ready for that yet.

"I have friends staying with me," he answered.

He then began to get dressed and squeezed passed me very quickly out the door. I thought he left. So I finished getting dressed, and then pushed open the door to leave.

We had been upstairs in the dark for a while because the light in the bar was very bright in my eyes and blinded me. I looked down to watch my step. When I looked up I saw him squatting down with his elbows resting on his knees and his fingers intertwined. He was looking up at me with a radiant smile. His eyes seemed to shine a beautiful blue like a calm ocean moving peacefully as the sun reflects off its movements. And there was joy beaming from them for the moment of seeing each other clearly for the first time.

It revealed a romantic side of him, the way he left the dark room so quickly without a word. He wanted to be ready for *that* moment. The first moment we would see each other, to be the first thing that I saw, and to see me for the first time as I came out of the dark. He was like an angel from Amsterdam.

And I realized it was the same man. The one with the blue knit cap and bits of blond hair peeking from underneath I had admired from atop my Juliet balcony at Havana's.

The one that I wanted to get to know.

The one that I got to know—in an unconventional way—was Love's invitation.

But I did not feel love for myself and would still need time to discover it on my own. So I kissed him and walked out the door, continuing on the road of choosing a new adventure. A gay adventure.

A couple years later when I found that love in myself, I was reminded of the Amsterdam Angel.

You were right! Realizing the love I felt inside was the same I'd experienced in his arms. *This is love.* Such a shame, I never even asked his name. But I'll never forget the beautiful boy that unknowingly helped me to grow strong and thrive, just like the sunflowers long ago I watched with Joe in a magical backyard.

I recognize now that it's my story of first love.